Rudy

Skittles 2

Mark
Thanks for Reading!
Best Wishes!
Doug Chatman

THE CURSED BLESSING

VIGILANTE OF LORD'S TREASURES | DOUG CHATMAN

TATE PUBLISHING
AND ENTERPRISES, LLC

VoLt
Copyright © 2012 by Doug Chatman. All rights reserved.

No part of this publication may be reproduced, stored in a retrieval system or transmitted in any way by any means, electronic, mechanical, photocopy, recording or otherwise without the prior permission of the author except as provided by USA copyright law.

This novel is a work of fiction. Names, descriptions, entities, and incidents included in the story are products of the author's imagination. Any resemblance to actual persons, events, and entities is entirely coincidental.

The opinions expressed by the author are not necessarily those of Tate Publishing, LLC.

Published by Tate Publishing & Enterprises, LLC
127 E. Trade Center Terrace | Mustang, Oklahoma 73064 USA
1.888.361.9473 | www.tatepublishing.com

Tate Publishing is committed to excellence in the publishing industry. The company reflects the philosophy established by the founders, based on Psalm 68:11,
"The Lord gave the word and great was the company of those who published it."

Book design copyright © 2012 by Tate Publishing, LLC. All rights reserved.
Cover design by Brandon Land
Interior design by Chelsea Womble

Published in the United States of America

ISBN: 978-1-62024-054-0
Fiction / Action & Adventure
12.05.25

ACKNOWLEDGMENTS

Thank you to Mom and Dad, who gave me an amazing childhood full of adventures and opportunities to use my imagination.

Thank you to my wife, Kim, for your love and encouraging support throughout this journey.

To Derek, Anna, Alec, and Kaden. You guys are my greatest accomplishments, even if it appears I don't know what I'm doing most of the time.

And to God be the glory, Great things He hath done! Thank you for placing this story on my heart. I immensely enjoyed watching it play out on numerous yellow note pads, and finally on my PC, where I witnessed the story write itself.

CHAPTER 1

The only source of light came from a single white candle on the dresser that flickered soft shadows on the walls of the small basement chamber. Dustin knelt at his bed, his black, woolen cloak spread out around, covering him. His hands tightly clasped together as the minutes ticked by. This twenty-five-year-old man searched for the right words to pray. His heart raced, his fingers turned white, and his forehead beaded with perspiration. Anxiety consumed him.

A drop of sweat trickled down his cheek only to be absorbed by the hood of his cloak. His legs cramped as he struggled with his conscience. Should he pray for strength? Guidance? Protection? Then it came to him.

"Please, Lord, forgive me for what I'm about to do, if it's not Your will. For in Your name I pray, amen."

Dustin attempted to release the tension by running his fingers through his thick, dark-brown hair. He stood up from his aching knees and walked over to the dresser. He placed his hands on the furniture piece. Allowing his knees to readjust, he gazed into the mirror. His green eyes stood out in contrast to his pale face, and he began to accept the realization of his impending action.

"Okay, let's make what's wrong, right," Dustin said to his reflection.

Reaching into his cloak's pocket, Dustin pulled out a long necklace made of a strip of leather. He held it up, gazing at the object dangling from it. A *V*-shaped medallion of gold gleamed in the candlelight. He fastened the necklace around his neck, allowing the medallion to rest on his bare chest.

From the moment the cold, gold element touched his exposed torso, he felt his body transform. His blood warmed as it flowed through his veins, reaching all extremities. His arms began to enlarge in size and length. The muscles in his body swelled and tightened. His back hunched over just as he experienced the explosion of rapid hair growth all over his body. He felt the muscles in his jaw and nose stretch as an ape-like snout began to form. Around his face and neck grew a dark-brown mane like that of a lion.

Knowing the monstrous transformation had completed, he fought the urge to look at himself in the mirror again. Quick and powerfully, he blew out the candle. Reaching over, he pulled the dresser back from the wall, revealing a small door. Only being four feet tall, the door hid perfectly behind the dresser. The doorway opened to a secret, dark tunnel. The beastly Dustin bent down, just barely clearing the petite doorframe and disappearing into the darkness.

Moments later, Dustin reemerged from the darkness along the side of the London underground subway tunnel. Hearing a fast-approaching train, he readied himself, poised to jump. As the last subway car approached, Dustin leaped with all his strength, landing on top of the moving car. His weight and the force of his landing caused the train car to rock back and forth, catching the passengers off guard as they quickly grabbed at the railings and seats. Dustin focused his energy on settling the car by using his weight to offset the rocking.

The train whizzed along as he felt the car settle down. All along, Dustin did his best to estimate his location on the subway's route. His newly improved eyesight recognized an opening to a small tunnel that would lead him close to where he needed to go.

"Here's my stop," Dustin said to himself.

He leaped from the car and landed on the small walkway edge that ran along the subway corridor. Looking up at the rapidly fading subway car, he saw the car rock back and forth again from the jolt of his departure.

"I'll have to work on that," he muttered.

Dustin began traveling along the nearly pitch-black walkway that eventually led him to a sewer tunnel. The stench of the sewer would be pungent to the average nose, but his newly acquired physique came with an enhanced ability of smell that nearly brought the mighty beast to his knees.

Eager to leave the sewer, he moved quickly, peering through gutters and spillways that emptied from the streets above. Fortunately, he spotted the landmark he wanted—the Fitzgerald Library. The ringing of distant church bells indicated that it was nine o'clock.

"Right on time," Dustin said.

Peering from the sewer, he stayed transfixed on the steps of the library that he could see clearly through the street gutter.

Dustin knew that a young man would eventually come out of the library. He just hoped he wasn't too late. As he pondered his timing, Dustin recognized a figure quickly making his way down the steps with his backpack strapped tightly over his shoulder. His raised shoulders and folded arms, along with his fast pace, indicated that the young man might have been nervous and scared.

Dustin watched the scrawny teenager walk down the moderately populated sidewalk, only glancing up occasionally to avoid bumping into others but mainly trying to avoid eye contact with everyone. As he began to walk out of Dustin's sight, the creature quickly looked for a manhole cover that he could crawl out of undetected.

The young man walked in front of a dark alleyway when he heard the voice that noticeably caught him off guard.

"Well, well, well, right on time again, Cameron, my little friend!" announced a thuggish teenager who was accompanied by two other hoodlums.

"I swear, Cam, I could literally set my clock by you, if I had one," he said, laughing at his own joke.

"Please, I don't have anything tonight, Kevin," Cameron pleaded. "You took all I had the last time."

"Well, you'll just have to pay another way then, eh?"

Kevin's two toadies, Cass and Chet, grabbed Cameron, dragging him down the alley.

"Please don't! I have to meet my mom!" Cameron pleaded.

"Oh! I'm sorry. Is this the point where I'm supposed to care?" Kevin said. "'Cause I don't."

Kevin motioned to his buddies to hold him up so he could get a clear shot at his gut.

Kevin swung back his arm with his fist ready to deliver a hard blow, when he felt someone grab his cocked wrist.

"Hey, what gives?" Kevin questioned angrily.

Turning around, he found himself face to face with a large, hairy, monstrous creature wearing a thick, black, hooded cape along with a gold *V* medallion around its neck that somehow shined in the dark alley.

"I think he wants you to let him go!" growled the beastly Dustin.

Cass and Chet released their grip on Cameron and jumped back in shock. Kevin stood horror-stricken as the creature faced him.

"Don't…don't hurt me!" Kevin pleaded.

"I'm sorry, is this where I'm supposed to care?" the monster taunted.

With one swing of his arm, the powerful beast sent Kevin flying back onto a trash dumpster. The impact knocked him out as he rolled and fell to the ground. Then the monster walked over to the two bullies, who were still standing motionless. Placing a hand on each of their heads, he rammed them together. The two dropped like sacks of cement.

The daunting monster turned his attention back to a woozy Kevin, who struggled to get to his feet. The beastly figure walked over to Kevin and, with one arm, picked him up and stared into his eyes. The creature could see the red glow of evil in them. With his other arm, the monstrous Dustin placed his hand over Kevin's face.

"Repent!" the creature growled.

Dustin could feel the evil leave Kevin's body and enter his own. The beast instantly felt the evil boil in his stomach. He dropped Kevin from his clutches and doubled over in sickness and gagged himself, allowing the release of the bile through his mouth. The creature stood upright and wiped the remnants from his mouth with his right hand. Shaking the drops of vomit from his hand, he reached in his pocket and pulled out a match. He struck the match against the building. Once the match was lit, he dropped it onto the bile, causing it to ignite into a rolling ball of fire that rapidly burned out with an evil hiss. Kevin sat on the ground in awe to what had transpired before him. Then Dustin slowly walked back over to Kevin, glaring at him.

"Go, and repeat this sin no more!"

Kevin jumped to run but stopped and looked at Cameron, who was curled up in a ball on the ground.

"Sorry, Cam, it won't happen again. I promise!" he said.

Kevin then looked down at Cass and Chet as they tried to shake the cobwebs out of their heads. A noticeable look of disgust showed on his face at the realization of the poor company he had been keeping. He shook his head no in a manner that he stated he didn't want to be around them anymore. He turned and ran away as fast as he could.

Then the beastly Dustin looked over at Cameron, whose noticeable quivering indicated that he thought he was the creature's next victim.

"You better hurry. Your mom will be waiting on you. You don't want her to worry," the monster said to Cameron.

"Huh?" Cameron responded.

"Go!" the monster barked.

Cameron jumped to his feet, quickly bent down to pick up his backpack, and proceeded to run out of the alley only to stop and look back at the creature.

Dustin began feeling annoyed with the young man's failure to follow a simple request.

"Thank you!" Cameron said softly. "And God bless."

Then he took off in a sprint to meet his mother.

"Boy, I hope He will, kid," the monstrous Dustin said as he leaned his back to the wall. Letting out a sigh of relief, he said to himself, "Not too bad for a first night on the job."

CHAPTER 2

Dustin woke up in his bed, his nightclothes damp from sweat. The sheets and covers were pulled and twisted. One leg lay exposed while the other was wrapped tightly in the bedding. Looking around the room, he stretched his arms out and arched his back. Feeling the acute soreness in his muscles, his thoughts went back to the previous night's events. He had a hard time believing that it had actually occurred.

I can only hope things will be easier for Cameron now, he thought.

Lying there, Dustin tried to plan the day in his head.

"What time is it anyway?" Dustin grumbled, looking at his digital alarm clock on the nightstand next to his bed. His eyes focused on the red glow of the numbers.

"Nine-thirty."

Dustin had overslept by an hour. He twisted under the covers, trying to get his mind and body to work in unison before attempting to get out of bed. Suddenly, a frightening thought came to him. What if he didn't transform back completely? Jumping up and running to the dresser, he checked his reflection. Dustin let out a sigh of relief, happy to see his own regular, plain image staring back at him.

Dustin leaned against the four-foot-high dresser. His hands grasping onto each side with the fingers curled around the edge as he supported his own weight. Still feeling a little nauseous, he began to reflect on the journey that led him to this new, unique ability.

An ability, that's all Dustin could consider it at this moment.

His mind began to wander back just a few weeks ago when this journey began. In fact, it had all started in this very room.

Dustin came in as the newly hired youth minister at the Berthel Church. The congregation brought him in with hopes that the youth membership might increase. He accepted the position with the agreement he could be an on-site resident.

Dustin had led only three Bible study sessions when the burdens of a young man began to weigh heavy on his heart. Only two teenagers showed up to his Bible studies. They were Cameron and Abbey. Abbey, the head deacon's daughter, attended at her father's request. Cameron, a shy, insecure boy, attended as a way to take a break from studying and to kill time until his mother got off from work.

In the last session, Cameron broke down sobbing, divulging how he would be stopped on his way to meet his mom by a group of bullies who attended his school. There were three of them. Their lives consisted of being a nuisance to society and being a torment to Cameron. They had Cameron's pattern figured out, and they didn't waste an opportunity to take what they could from him, whether it was money or self-esteem.

Cameron's situation plagued Dustin's mind all night.

"Something needs to happen," Dustin said to himself several times that night as he tossed and turned in bed.

The next morning, he knelt down at his bed and began to pray.

"Dear Lord, God Almighty, grant me the guidance to lead others to Christ and help me to be a positive influence not only in the church but in the community." He paused as he tried to be more direct in his prayer. "And dear Lord, I lift up Cameron to you. Allow your grace to flow on him and ease the burdens that are plaguing his life."

While Dustin was in deep meditation, allowing God to speak to his heart, his senses became aware of a slight breeze flowing through his room. The distraction was not enough to interfere, but nonetheless, he was aware of it.

"…in your name I pray…Amen."

Dustin stood up to stretch his legs and arms. As he relaxed, he again became aware of the small breeze flowing through the room. He found it odd since both his door and window were closed. He began trying to follow the breeze with his hand. His search led him to his dresser.

Examining the dresser, he could tell the breeze came from behind it. He attempted to move the old, walnut furniture, but it wouldn't move. Kneeling down, he examined the bottom of it. He could tell that it hadn't been moved in some time. Dustin mustered all his strength and attempted to move the dresser again. Gritting his teeth, and pushing against it, and with a noticeable *pop*, it broke loose from years of grime and dirt.

Dustin stood there, studying his findings. Before him was a small door about four feet tall and three feet wide, just small enough to be completely hidden behind the dresser. The top of the door appeared to be about two feet below ground level, according to Dustin's best estimation.

Looking around the room, making sure no one was watching him, he grabbed the door to open it, but it too was glued shut with years of muck.

Curiosity had the best of him. Dustin needed to know what hid behind this door. He stood there for a moment looking around his room for something to pry the door open with. Nothing in his quarters would suffice. He walked out his room and walked down the hallway to the janitor closet. Opening the door, he reached and pulled the string, allowing the light to click on. Glancing around the closet, he found a screwdriver and flashlight sitting on one of the shelves. Dustin grabbed the two items and quickly dashed back to his room.

Dustin studied the door and wedged the tip of the screwdriver into the frame, prying it. The door popped open with a loud thump. Dustin sat still for a moment, wondering if anybody heard it. Slowly, he peered inside the entry and discovered that the small door led to a shallow, dark tunnel.

Dustin grabbed the flashlight and switched it on and cautiously entered the tunnel. He had to brush away numerous cobwebs as the tunnel led him sharply downward. Dustin's feet slid along the soft, dirt path as the amber light led him down about fifty feet. He managed to stop his slide at the bottom of the passageway. To his surprise, the tunnel opened into a larger corridor that ran north and south, parallel to the church above. Studying the large corridor, he found it to be arched with partial tiling on the lower portions of the wall. He realized that he found an unfinished vein of the underground subway system. Looking down the corridor to the left, he could see that it only extended fifteen feet where the construction ended, but it extended to the right about twice as far, where it was sealed off from a finished subway tunnel.

Dustin walked down to the sealed-off wall and saw flashes of light coming from the small opening in the makeshift manhole cover door, which stayed in place on the angled-out wall. The flickering glow came from a subway train passing by.

"Hummm…" Dustin said, pleased with his discovery.

Grabbing the sides of the tunnel, he struggled to make his way back up the corridor to his room. As he approached the small door, his flashlight exposed something above a support beam just inside the tunnel outside his door. It was an old, wooden crate. Dustin reached up to pull it down only to find the crate wedged in pretty tight. After a couple of minutes of pulling and tugging, the crate finally broke free. He carried the crate back into his quarters and placed it on the floor in the middle of room. He pushed the dresser back, completely covering the secret door.

Dustin quickly dashed to the bathroom across the hall to wash his hands of the mud he accumulated on his journey, eager to investigate what he found.

Once he made it back to his room, he knelt down and began to open the crate. The lid of the box had weakened over the years and popped off rather easily. Inside, he found some old paper clippings and an old, gold pocket watch.

The watch was well crafted with a detailed, engraved design on the lid. He managed to open the pocket watch with his thumbnail. Inside, besides the clock face, was a black-and-white photograph of a woman who appeared to be in her twenties.

Wow, she's pretty, Dustin thought.

After studying the image and the antique timepiece, he glanced over the aged newspaper clippings. They were dated within the years 1940 and 1941.

"That was during the beginning of World War II," he said to himself.

The articles reported on sightings of a person or creature of some sort. They indicated that, at first, the creature was thought to be feared, but later articles reported that the creature appeared to assist in the rescue of a family and the arrest of a bank robber.

At the top of each article, someone had written, "Make what is wrong, right."

"Strange," Dustin concluded.

Dustin gathered the clippings and placed them in the bottom drawer of his dresser. Then he grabbed the antique timepiece and placed it in his pocket. His findings had him intrigued.

Dustin glanced at his watch. "Holy cow!" he said out loud. "I'm five minutes late!"

His shift started at nine o'clock. Dustin trotted up the stairs and jogged to the sanctuary where he saw Reverend Phillips speaking to the church secretary, Sharon.

The head pastor was a middle-aged man with hint of gray in his thick, jet-black hair. He stood a couple inches taller than Dustin, which made it easier for him not only to look to Phillips as a superior but also as a father figure.

"My apologies, Reverend," Dustin said. "Time kind of got away from me."

"Not a problem, Dustin," Reverend Phillips replied.

"While I have both of you here, can I ask you two a question?" Dustin requested.

"Sure, what is it?" the reverend returned the question.

"I found some articles that might have belonged to whoever lived in my quarters long before me. Would anybody here be able to tell me who they might belong to?" Dustin asked.

"What kind of articles?" asked the redheaded secretary.

"Well, the most important one would be this pocket watch I found," Dustin said as he pulled it out of his pocket.

Both the reverend and Sharon studied the timepiece.

"Oh my, that's very pretty!" Sharon remarked. "Is there a picture inside?"

"Yes, there is." Dustin answered as he opened up the antique, revealing a picture of the girl. "Do you recognize her?" he asked the two of them.

"No, I sure don't," replied Sharon. "But you know, there is one person here that might know who lived in your quarters, and she even might know who that is in that picture."

"Really?" Dustin replied with raised eyebrows.

"Yes, her name is Miss Parsons," Sharon answered.

"Any chance that she'll be here this Sunday?" Dustin asked.

The pastor and Sharon looked at each other and smiled.

"Oh, she'll be here all right. Come rain, sleet, snow, or shine, she'll be here," the reverend said. "She never misses a Sunday."

———————————

Sunday morning came, and Dustin took his regular spot on the second pew. So eager to meet Miss Parsons, Dustin couldn't even recall what the sermon was about. When the sermon began to conclude with the invitation, Dustin made his way to the back of the church, hoping to catch Miss Parsons before she left. He greeted the church members as they filed out. Curiosity got the best of him when Sharon came to the door.

"Which one is she?" he asked her. It took a moment for Sharon to recall their previous conversation.

Sharon looked around the sanctuary and spotted Miss Parsons sitting in her normal spot. She always sat in the right side pew, eight rows from the front.

"There she is," Sharon said while pointing towards her. "Good Luck."

"Thanks!" Dustin said as he headed in her direction before Sharon could finish her sentence.

As he approached her, he saw that she was an elderly woman. Quickly doing the math in his head, he estimated her to be in her mid-eighties. Dustin studied her as he approached. She had a small frame but appeared to be in relatively good shape for a woman of her age. Her full head of gray was done up in a bun. He watched her put on her white sweater over her blue dress lined in white lace as he drew near.

"Excuse me, ma'am, but—" he started to introduce himself, but she held up her hand before he could finish his introduction.

"I know exactly who you are, Mr. Dustin Albatrose," she said with a smile. "You're the new youth minister."

"Well, yes I am," he responded with a pleasant smile. "It's nice to meet you."

Dustin extended his hand as she gently reached out and shook it.

"It's nice to meet you too, young man."

"I was wondering if you could help me with something?" he asked.

"Certainly, I'm here to serve," she answered with a genuine smile.

"Thank you," Dustin replied as he released the handshake and reached in his pocket to retrieve the pocket watch. "I found some items in my living quarters. Sharon, our church secretary, indicated that you might be able to shed some light on who used to live there?"

Opening his palm and displaying the old watch, he gestured for her to take a look at it. She slowly reached in and picked it up. She held the timepiece in the palm of her hand and sat back down as she gazed at the antique watch. Dustin looked for an expression on her face, and his heart sank when he noticed tears welling up in her eyes. She just sat there, caressing the watch over and over. They sat there for a while in silence.

Then she finally looked up at Dustin and said, "It's been such a long time since I last saw this watch."

She opened it to find the picture inside, and she smiled a tearful smile.

"You know who that is?" Dustin asked.

"Why, yes I do," she answered with a smile. "It's me."

CHAPTER 3

Dustin took Miss Parsons out to lunch to the little café across the street. They sat inside at a small table in front of the window. The establishment was filled with other church members who were enjoying lunch and socializing with each other. As Miss Parsons and Dustin tried to drown out the crowd, she went on to tell him of the events that occurred in the fall of 1940.

She informed him that a young man had arrived at the church to be the new youth minister. His name was Tim Warner. Just like Dustin, he was a recent graduate from the seminary, and Berthel Church was his first hired position.

"I was just a couple of years out of high school myself, but I stayed active in the church and in the community. With the war going on, I just felt the need to stay close," she said between sips of her tea.

"Since I was familiar with most of the youth in the church, I volunteered to help Tim become acquainted with the youth." A smile came to her face as she reminisced. "A friendship quickly emerged, but to be honest with you, I felt more than just friendship," she said with a shy, guilty smile.

Dustin returned the smile to her.

"We soon admitted we had feelings for each other, but issues began to arise—issues that started outside of us," she said.

"What kind of issues?" Dustin asked.

She paused and then softly shook her head no, as if she didn't want to mention it.

"Anyway, I gave that pocket watch to Tim the last night I saw him. It broke my heart when he left, and it breaks again knowing he didn't take it with him."

She stopped speaking and stared at her coffee cup.

Dustin felt horrible. He thought he was doing some good after seeing her face light up as she spoke fondly of her time with Tim. But the reality that Tim might not have felt the same way about her left a noticeable deep void in her expression.

"Do you know what happened to Tim?" he asked.

"Well," she answered, swallowing her held back tears. "I heard he joined the military soon after he left the church. After the war, he went home to the family farm in Jennings in the northern country. From what I understand, he's still working on the farm."

"Did you ever try to contact him?" he asked.

"Yes, but the attempts were never returned," she replied.

Dustin went on asking about what she had done since then. He felt shocked and disappointed to find out that she never really recovered from the broken heart that Tim had caused. A strong sense of unresolved business hung in the air as Miss Parsons concluded her story. Questions about Tim's rationality began to build in Dustin's mind. He tried to not to come to premature conclusions about Tim. Miss Parsons seemed to be a true, genuine, sweet person. Why she couldn't recover from Tim was a question Dustin couldn't find the answer to.

Regardless, it just didn't seem fair for Miss Parsons to deny herself the opportunity to fall in love again. Dustin felt agitation towards Tim at the thought that Tim had robbed her of potentially having a long, happy life. He wanted to travel to the northern country and attempt to meet and visit with Tim Warner, hoping that he would find the answers that have mounted ever since he found the old, gold pocket watch.

"Well, I thank you for lunch. It was awfully nice to finally meet you," Miss Parsons said with a genuine smile.

Dustin quickly stood up as Miss Parsons got up from the table.

"The pleasure was all mine," he replied. "And Miss Parsons, let me know if there's anything I can do."

Miss Parsons smiled and nodded in appreciation. Dustin sat back down as he watched her leave and make her way down the sidewalk towards her home. He sat there for a moment, going over the conversation in his head.

Dustin made his way back to the church, where he ran into the pastor just as he was leaving.

"Did you enjoy your luncheon with Miss Parson?" the minister asked.

"Uh, yes I did, but I feel that there are many unresolved issues."

"Anything we can do about it?" Pastor Phillips asked.

Dustin shrugged his shoulders. "I don't know. She indicated that Mr. Warner might live in the northern country."

"Mr. Warner?" Phillips asked.

"Yes, Tim Warner. He's the gentleman that lived in the apartment during the early nineteen-forties. Evidently, he and Miss Parsons had feelings for each other. And without much warning, he just left one night."

"Hmmm…" the minister said, shaking his head slightly while rubbing his chin with his right arm. "Do you know where Mr. Warner is?"

"She said he's working on the family farm a few miles outside of Jennings," Dustin replied.

"Well, I guess you could always travel up there and see if you can find any answers," Phillips suggested.

Dustin couldn't believe his ears. He had been tossing around the idea of possibly traveling to the Warner family farm, but he thought that the pastor would think he was out of his mind for planning such an expedition. But now, the proposal was on the table, delivered by Pastor Phillips himself.

"Really? That would be great," Dustin replied.

"Very good then. Take a couple of days this week and make the trip. I'll lead your Bible study group on Wednesday while you're gone," Phillips said.

"Thank you, sir. Thank you very much for understanding," Dustin replied, shaking the pastor's hand with gratitude.

Dustin made his way back to his quarters. He felt a huge burden lifted from his shoulders. Normally, if he were to make a decision like this on his own, the voices of doubt in his head would have him rethinking his decision. But since the reverend suggested it, Dustin didn't have to carry that load on his own.

CHAPTER 4

The train crept into the depot and jerked to a stop. Dustin felt his body rock back and forth along with the other passengers.

"Penrith," the recorded voice announced.

Dustin stood and grabbed his brown leather duffle bag from the empty seat next to him and swung it over his shoulder. Walking over to the door, he glanced through the window at the scenery before him. He could see a small, self-sufficient city—nothing near the size of London that he had become accustomed to. A steady rain soured his anxious mood. He zipped up his navy-blue jacket and popped open his black umbrella as he stepped from the train.

"Excuse me," he said as he noticed that a couple had to walk around him while he stood on the platform, getting his bearings on his location.

Finding the depot office, he walked over, doing his best to avoid the puddles. He stopped under the awning and shook the umbrella and collapsed it. He then proceeded in.

"I need a taxi to take me to Jennings," Dustin said to the man behind the counter.

"Jennings? That's a good little drive," the train clerk responded with a quick judgment. "Around the corner, you'll find a line of them. Good luck finding one that will take you there."

"Thanks," Dustin said as he turned around towards the door while slightly rolling his eyes.

He walked outside and around the corner as the depot attendant had directed him. He found four taxis lined up ready for hire. Dustin tapped on the first cab's window. The driver rolled the window just enough to let Dustin speak to him.

"Jennings?" he asked.

The taxi driver shook his head no while mumbling something that Dustin couldn't understand, and the window quickly rolled up.

Dustin proceeded to the next taxi and received the same response. The third cab laughed when he heard Dustin's destination.

"Jennings? Go fish!" The driver laughed as he thumbed Dustin back to try the last cab.

Another sign? If he was meant to be here, then why all the signs that he shouldn't be? The long train ride, the rain, the unwilling cab drivers, and the negative attitudes—all excuses running through his mind, any excuse that would give him just cause to get back on the train and go home. The doubts that questioned his every decision were never far away.

By the time Dustin already approached the last cab, his mood was as dreary as the day. The man already had his window cracked, waiting to hear where Dustin wanted to go.

"Where to, lad?" the driver asked.

"Jennings?" Dustin asked again.

The man smiled and rubbed his two-day beard as if he enjoyed plays of the secret taxi game that he and his fellow cab drivers were participating in.

"Jennings, huh? Okay, I'm game. Hop on in."

"Really?"

Dustin could feel his eyes pop open in surprise that he finally found someone willing to take him. He jumped in the back seat and again shook off the umbrella before collapsing it and shutting the door.

"Are you from Jennings?" the man asked.

"No, I'm on a wild goose chase, you could say."

"Well, it must be some kind of chase if it takes you to Jennings."

"What is it about the town?"

"Oh, mostly urban legends. You know, ghosts and goblins."

"Great," Dustin said as the cab drove off into the distance with the doubts not far behind.

The taxi made its way through the wooded territory. Dustin stared off into the passing forest, collecting his thoughts and courage with each passing mile. For a moment or two, he thought he saw shadows jumping back and forth behind the trees. He attributed to the "ghost-and-goblin" theory his driver had referred to earlier.

Just as his eyelids started to feel like weights, the taxi came into the clearing, showing the small town of Jennings before them.

"Here you go, lad," the driver said. "Jennings."

Dustin sat up in his seat and peered out the front windshield, taking in the view of the town. It did seem small—perhaps a population of three hundred by the number of houses he could see.

The cab pulled up to the gas station located at the entrance of the town and stopped. Dustin looked up and read the meter and pulled out the bills from his back pocket. The driver continued to look around as if he were rather anxious to head out as soon as possible.

"Here you go," Dustin said as he reached through the partition window and handed the driver the fare along with a tip.

"Thanks, lad! Good luck to you. I'm afraid you're gonna need it."

"Thanks," Dustin replied in a deflated tone.

Dustin crawled out of the car and proceeded to shut the door behind him, but the cab was already moving before he had a chance to close it. He stood there and watched the taxi drive off and quickly disappear into the wooded landscape.

Quiet. That was Dustin's first observation of the town—quiet. He walked over and made his way to the two-pump gas station and stepped into the store. An overweight, sixty-something gentleman sat behind the counter on a pub stool, reading the *London Times*. The clerk looked over his reading glasses without moving his head at Dustin as he approached the counter.

"Can I help you?" the clerk asked.

"Uh, yes," Dustin said as he tightened the strap over his shoulder. "I'm looking for the Warner farm. Do you know where I might find it?"

"The Warner farm—what business brings you there?"

Dustin was caught off guard with the question to his question. He just wanted to know the location of the farm. He didn't know why he had to explain himself to everyone he encountered.

"An old-time correspondent, I guess," he answered as he slightly lifted his eyebrows, as if hoping that would be a good enough answer for the man.

"Ah, okay. Well, you'll have to travel back up the road you just came from."

Dustin shifted and turned slightly to look up the same road out the window.

"About a twenty-minute walk. You'll find the entrance on your right. It winds back a bit, but you'll know it when you see it."

"Twenty-minute walk?" Dustin said.

He started to notice the emptiness in his stomach. He knew he didn't have the energy to walk that far at this moment.

"Anywhere around here I could grab a bite?"

The clerk smiled and pointed to the various chips and candy bar shelves in front of him.

"I guess that will do," he said as he started looking for his lunch.

CHAPTER 5

Dustin followed the aged wooden fence alongside the road until he reached the entrance to the farm. He stood at the entrance for a moment as he gazed at the drive that led up to the farmhouse that looked to be another two hundred yards away. Mustering all the strength and confidence he had, he followed the worn-out tire tracks up to the house. With each step, he could feel the voice of doubt questioning this venture. He thought about praying, but the fact that he thought about praying gave him enough justification that he didn't have to.

Dustin studied the red-brown, brick house hidden behind a couple of sparsely planted, mature trees as he approached the residence. There wasn't a fancy front porch to welcome visitors, just three cement blocks that served as steps to the side door. Cautiously, Dustin knocked on the door. The metal screen door shook and rattled with each knock. He paused and waited for a moment. He didn't want to appear to be snooping by looking through the nearby windows, so he focused his attention on the screen door in front of him. After counting to ten, he knocked again. Finally, a shadow could be seen approaching the door.

The door opened out a foot while a woman who appeared to be in her early thirties peered out cautiously and looked at Dustin. "Can I help you?" she asked, looking skeptically at the stranger as she wiped her hands with a kitchen wash cloth.

"Uh, yes. First, I apologize for the interruption, but could you tell me if I could find a Mister Tim Warner here?" Dustin asked.

"Uncle Tim?" she responded.

"Uh, maybe?"

She paused for a second as if trying to decide Dustin's intentions behind his sudden appearance.

"What do you want with Uncle Tim?" the woman asked. He was so close to finding him, yet he knew the wrong response might end his search. He hoped just the simple truth would be enough to let him pass this guardian of Tim's.

"Well, I came across some of his belongings in my apartment. I just felt the need to return them to their rightful owner," Dustin explained.

"What are you, a priest?" she asked sarcastically as she stepped outside and walked down the steps to ground level.

"Close, a youth minster."

She looked at him with a double take and stood there in front of him with her arms folded.

"Where are you from exactly?"

"London. More specifically, the Berthel Church, where your uncle used to be the youth minister," Dustin said.

By the look on her face, this was news to her. The questions stopped. Shaking her head slightly in disbelief, she started walking back to the barn.

"He should be back here," she said as she continued walking without really giving an invitation to Dustin to follow her. Nonetheless, Dustin decided to follow her back to the barn. They walked in an awkward silence. When they finally reached the large, gray, wooden structure, she turned to Dustin and said, "Wait here a moment."

She made her way back to where he could see a silhouette of a man that appeared to be tossing hay into the pin where sheep had arrived to eat. Dustin tried his best to eavesdrop on their conversation, but the wind that whipped around the farm drowned them out. An uneasiness came over Dustin as he saw the shadowy figure look in his direction. Dustin could tell he was being sized up. After a couple of awkward moments, the figure gestured to the woman as if saying he wasn't interested in what Dustin had to sell.

The woman approached Dustin with her orders.

"Uncle Tim said that whatever you found, you can keep," she said. "Sorry you came all this way for nothing, but Uncle Tim isn't entertaining guests today."

Dustin couldn't believe his ears. He hadn't traveled all this way only to be stopped at the verge of having all of these questions answered. With a rapid sense of agitation welling up inside him, he stopped and stood still directly in front of her.

"Are you telling me I can't speak to him?" he asked.

"I'm afraid so," she replied.

"I need to ask him about some things."

"I'm sorry, but he's not in the mood right now," she responded as she gestured with her arm that he needed to proceed back down the drive and back down the road.

Dustin frantically ran through his mind for something to do or say. Then it came to him. Dustin turned around and held his hands to his mouth in an attempt to direct his voice in Tim's direction.

"I just want to make what's wrong right! At least that's what Jessica would want me to do!"

Dustin's heart raced at his own bold attempt to get Mr. Warner's attention.

Nobody moved. The woman stood in shock over Dustin's shouting. Dustin stood frozen as he watched the distant figure stop his feeding and stand still while the words echoed over the farm. Then slowly, the figured laid the rake against the building and began approaching Dustin.

Dustin's heart raced more. Now he wanted to pray, but he couldn't come up with the words.

The shadowy figure came out of the darkness. Dustin could clearly see an eighty-year-old man approach him. But Mr. Warner did not move like someone of that age. His mobility and posture mimicked someone much younger. Gray hairs streaked the sides of his head but continued to battle with his brown hair on top. He had the normal wrinkles that Dustin expected, but a good majority of the creases on his face were due to the scowl he had directed at Dustin. Dustin held his breath as Tim walked up to him.

"Who did you say you were again?" Tim asked.

"I'm...I'm Dustin Albatrose. The youth minister from Berthel Church," Dustin answered as if answering a general in the army.

"What did you find exactly?" Tim asked.

"I found this gold pocket watch," Dustin quickly answered as he dug through his backpack and found the timepiece. Finding it, he handed it over to Tim. Tim took it from Dustin's hand. Slowly, Tim opened the pocket watch and found the picture inside still intact. Tim stood silently as he studied the picture.

"Miss Parsons told me it was her in the picture," Dustin said.

Tim quickly snapped his head up to look Dustin in the eyes.

"Jessica? She's still alive?" Tim asked.

"Yeah, attends service every Sunday," Dustin answered. "You know, I don't think she ever got over you."

"Likewise," Tim responded as he stared in her black-and-white image.

The tension began to subside between Dustin and Tim. Dustin looked up to see Tim's niece still standing there as if waiting for her next orders.

"It's okay, Maggie. Everything's fine," Tim said.

"Okay, just let me know if you need anything," she answered as she slowly turned around to head back to the house but not without giving Dustin one more glare.

"Thank you," Dustin said to Maggie as she walked away. "Tough crowd," he quietly said to himself.

Tim led Dustin back to the barn where he brushed off an old bar stool for Dustin to sit on at the workbench that ran alongside the wall. Tim walked over and sat on his own stool and turned around and placed the pocket watch on the bench as he studied it.

"So, how is she?" Tim asked.

"She's well and very charming—a true servant of God," Dustin replied.

"Yep, that sounds like Jessica."

"I don't mean to be blunt, but can I ask you why you left the way you did back in 1941?" Dustin asked.

Tim shifted his head slightly to look at Dustin out of the corners of his eye.

"It's complicated," Tim said, turning his attention back to Jessica's picture.

"I'm sure it is, but if you truly love someone, couldn't something be worked out?"

"Son, you weren't there. There were too many variables. It was for her own good that I left," Tim responded.

"Did it have something to do with these articles?" Dustin said as he pulled out the news clippings from his backpack.

"You found these?" Tim asked.

"Yeah, behind that small door that was hidden behind the dresser," Dustin explained.

"How did you find it?"

"Well, I was praying one day, and I felt a breeze coming from behind the dresser. I found the door, then I found the tunnel, then I came across the crate."

Tim sat quietly as if pondering all the events that had transpired before him.

"So, what do these articles have to do with anything?" Dustin asked, breaking the eerie silence.

Tim continued to sit in silence. Then he turned and looked at Dustin. Dustin could see an internal struggle going on behind Tim's eyes. He knew to sit quietly and wait for Tim's next move. Tim closed his eyes for a moment and then let out a long sigh.

"So, you want to know the story, the whole story?" Tim asked.

"Well, I did feel the need to track you down," Dustin answered.

"A need or a calling?"

"I do believe God sent me here," Dustin said.

"That's the scary part about answering God's calling. You never know where it's going to take you," Tim said.

As unsettling as the words seemed to be, to Dustin, they were true. Dustin had faith in God, but sometimes that blind faith could be a bit unnerving.

"You just have to keep the faith," Dustin said.

It appeared to be the answer that Tim needed to hear.

"Very well then," Tim said as he started reflecting to that time all those years ago. Tim continued as Dustin sat intently listening to the history lesson.

"I had just turned twenty-two and was fresh from graduating out the seminary in the spring of 1940. England was at war with Germany, and I had received my first assignment as the youth minister at Berthel Church…"

CHAPTER 6

The crisp, London wind collected leaves along the edges of the sidewalks and streets on that fall day in 1940. Tim Warner stood in his small apartment, looking out the ground-level window collecting his thoughts. With all of his belongings put away in his dresser, he was ready to begin his career in the youth ministry.

Dear Lord, I hope I'm ready for this.

Doubts consumed Tim's mind. Trying to put those negative thoughts in the back of his brain was a daily ritual. He had the training, the knowledge, and the calling. But that small voice kept whispering in his ear, *"You don't know what you're doing."*

Tim, recognizing the voice, quickly stopped and prayed. "Lord, I need you. Walk with me!"

Tim looked over his quaint, little room. A bed, a dresser, and a nightstand were all that took up the room, along with that small, four-foot door that appeared to lead to nothing.

Tim recalled asking about it when he first walked into his room. Pastor Canow told him it was where the coal used to be kept to heat the church. They had to lock it up because the city had been in the process of expanding the London underground subway just below them. The workers created a tunnel from the construction site to the coal shaft just outside that small door. They would use this as an easier means to get back and forth during the building of the subway vein. But funding for expansion had been stopped since the war began, and they recently learned that they were unable to finish this subway line due to budget problems and the poor stability of the area.

"That would be a great way to escape," Tim said, trying to amuse himself yet taking a mental note that it could be a true possibility.

Looking at his watch, he knew it was time to report. He couldn't put it off any longer.

Tim walked out of his living quarters. Taking a deep breath, he proceeded through the basement of the church to the front staircase that led to the building's foyer. Taking every bit of effort he had, Tim dragged himself upstairs to meet Pastor Canow in the sanctuary.

Hanging his lead low, Tim reached the top step. Suddenly someone in the foyer caught his attention. A young woman stood in the doorway of the sanctuary, her back turned to him. She had a small figure that was enhanced by her light-brown hair that flowed in waves down to her shoulders. While slowly moving toward her, he quickly had to remind himself to act respectfully to the ministry position in which he presided. Then, Tim noticed the sudden lack of breathing on his part as she turned around only to meet his wide-eyed, brown pupils. He studied her green eyes, her thin lips, and the cutest little freckles that lightly ran under her eyes and over her little nose.

Love, romance, dating…those were the last things on his mind prior to seeing her, but all of those emotions flooded his mind as if a dam that had just broken. He worked quickly to gain his mental composure as he approached her.

"Hello, I'm Tim Warner—" he said.

"Oh, you're the new youth minister!" she said, finishing his introduction for him.

"Uh, yes, I am. And you are?" he replied with a smile that matched hers.

"My name is Jessica Parsons," she answered. "We're really glad you're here!"

"Uh, thank you," he replied, being totally captivated by her presence.

He nervously ran his fingers through his freshly cut, brown hair. For a brief moment, he wondered if his five-foot nine-inch, skinny frame was as appealing to her as she was to him.

"I don't want you to think that I'm being too forward, but I know the youth really well. In fact, I have worked with them a lot, and I'd like to help you get acquainted with them if that's okay," she said.

Caught off guard by her offer of assistance, Tim knew it was too good to pass on, so he quickly accepted.

"That would be great! Wow, really, really great!"

Hearing his own words caused a small flush of embarrassment to come over him. He quickly refocused his mind on the true reason he was there, which was to serve God.

Jessica showed up at the very first youth meeting that Tim led. She made the transition easy for both Tim and the youth as they all got to know each other. Naturally, it didn't take long for a friendship to form between Tim and Jessica, but Tim had to admit to himself that he felt more than friendship budding.

Tim had been fortunate enough to keep in touch with a couple of his classmates from the seminary, Charles and Nancy. Charles and Nancy had met and begun dating during the last couple of years at the seminary. They were the "it couple" on campus. Charles, ruggedly handsome with blond hair and blue eyes, had an outgoing personality that complemented his talented musical skills. This made him the envy of every man on campus. Nancy, the equally attractive redhead, had a natural talent for singing.

The school looked down on their relationship. The administrators were a group of old men who thought that the student body of young twenty-year-olds should be focused only on God and his teachings and not romance. Charles and Nancy didn't let that stand in their way. Charles received his first assignment as the music director at the Webster Church. The church, only a twenty-minute walk from Tim's church, made it easy for the two to stay in contact. Nancy continued her search for a church position of her own. In the meantime, she found contentment as Charles's assistant. More importantly, she found happiness in just being able to be with him.

Tim would make a point to meet with his friends whenever the opportunity presented itself. The trio enjoyed many outings together, but unfortunately on occasion, the evening would be interrupted by air raids from the Germans.

The Nazi bombings over London struck terror across the city. Citizens would run for cover and hold their breath until the attacks were over. Some took cover in basements while others took shelter in the London underground subway system. Night after weary night, the Nazi air raids killed hundreds of innocent people and paralyzed thousands of others with fear. People did their best to go about their normal, daily lives, but the next air strike resided in the back of everyone's mind.

One night, Tim and his two friends were having dinner at a small café. It served as a good halfway point between the two residences. They sat at the darkly lit café, sipping tea and enjoying the light conversation among the other patrons who filled the establishment.

"So, Tim, are you becoming acquainted with anyone at your church?" Charles asked his friend.

"Yeah, sure. Everyone there is great," Tim said.

Tim knew what Charles was fishing for. Tim's love life, or lack thereof, was a regular topic to joke about. So naturally, Tim kept his hidden feelings for his new acquaintance a secret.

"Oh, well, give it time," Charles said, looking sorry for him. "Someone will come along."

"Yeah, maybe one of these days," Tim responded with an innocent smile.

Tim looked at his watch. It was ten after nine.

"Wow, look at the time. I better be going," Tim said as he stood from the table.

"Yep, we better be going too, my love," Nancy said. "Same time next week, Tim?" she asked.

"Sounds good!" Tim replied.

The three of them walked outside the café. Tim looked up at the starry, evening sky. England's normally cloudy climate kept the stars hidden most of the time. It wasn't very often that you could see the stars so well. Nancy looked up as well to the celestial display.

"What a lovely evening for a walk," Nancy said, filled with enthusiasm.

"It sure is!" Charles agreed as he put his arm around Nancy in her red plaid coat and squeezed her tight.

"Please, wait till I'm out of sight," Tim said with a smile.

Giving them both a friendly hug, he said, "I'll see you guys next week."

"Have a good week!" Charles said as they turned and made their way west back home.

Tim turned east and walked in the direction of his home. He enjoyed his quiet walks home by himself. He let his mind wander, reliving times at school and moments he had spent with Jessica. He noticed that when he thought about Jessica, he would catch himself smiling.

Tim made it three blocks from the café when he heard a distant hum coming from the skies. Just then, the air raid sirens began to wail. Tim's heart sank as the sound of the approaching Nazi airplanes grew louder and louder.

"Wow! They're close this time," Tim said.

He looked up. His heart jumped into his throat, and his legs felt numb. He could clearly see German airplanes flying over. One plane flew much lower than the others, with bombs in position to be dropped. He watched in horror as the plane flew over and witnessed the bombs fall from the plane's belly. Frozen with fear, he watched the bombs burst into fireballs off in the distance. Then he felt the echoed thunder of the explosion. His stomach sank, and he suddenly found himself running in the direction of the fiery sky.

CHAPTER 7

Tim stood in complete shock as he surveyed the neighborhood where he had been just minutes before. Smoke and flames engulfed buildings while piles of burning debris covered the streets. People could be heard screaming in pain and in horror. Men worked frantically to help those injured or trapped under the rubble.

Tim found himself drawn to one group of rescuers as they quickly dug to uncover someone trapped under a collapsed wall. As they pulled off the bricks and boards, Tim was horrified to recognize the coat of the individual under the bricks and concrete.

"Charles!" Tim shouted as he found himself pushing the other rescuers aside so he could reach his friend. Tim reached out to Charles as he saw his friend start to move around while trying to come out of the shock.

"Charles. It's me, Tim!" he said with Charles opening his eyes.

"Tim! Where's Nancy?" he asked frantically.

"I...uh...don't know?" Tim answered, fearing the worst for Nancy.

"We've got to find her!" Charles cried as he stumbled around.

A couple of unknown rescuers started helping Charles in his search for her. They worked feverishly to find her as they dug through the rumble. A man shouted, "I found something!"

The group quickly moved to the area of the possible find. Charles and Tim looked in horror as they recognized the red plaid coat that began to emerge from the rubble. Unable to move, the two watched as others freed Nancy from the debris. The rescuers laid her limp body on the ground.

One of the rescuers looked up at Charles and said, "I'm sorry, son."

Charles walked over to her and collapsed at her side and began to sob. Charles picked her up and cradled her against him. Tim walked over, knelt down, and placed his arm around Charles.

"Why? Why, God, Why?" he cried, rocking her back and forth. "No! No! No!"

Tim didn't say anything; he just knelt there rocking back and forth with Charles. Sirens of fire trucks and ambulances echoed around them, but neither one of them could hear them over the cries of Charles and the heartache that rang in their ears.

The next couple of weeks were long and painful for Charles following Nancy's funeral. Charles took a leave of absence from his duties at the church to deal with the mourning of his loss. Tim did his best in being there for Charles. Tim prayed to God to allow the pain to subside in Charles, but Tim noticed that Charles's pain was slowing turning into anger. With each bit of acceptance of Nancy's death, Charles's heart began to turn black with rage. Tim did everything he could to save his friend. Tim had difficulty finding the right words to say with each and every visit with Charles.

He would end his visits by telling Charles that he would continue praying for him. But in one visit, those words fell flat when Charles responded with, "Just keep your prayers to yourself."

"What do you mean, Charles?" Tim asked.

"Tim, if there truly is a God, then why would He take Nancy?" Charles replied.

"Sometimes God doesn't make sense," Tim responded, "but he always has a purpose for everything."

Charles rolled his eyes and smirked. "You know, Tim. I'm beginning to think that's nothing but rubbish." He paused. "Pure rubbish."

"You don't mean that," Tim replied.

"Oh yes, I do," Charles answered flatly. "Now, if you don't mind, I have some things I've got to do."

Tim left feeling helpless, knowing that he might have done more harm than good. He made his way home, replaying all of the events of the last exchange of words with Charles. He kept playing out different scenarios in his head, wondering what would have happened if he had said things differently, but each scenario turned out the same. Charles was not in the frame of mind to hear about God and His unconditional love. Tim decided to grant Charles his wish, and he gave him his space.

Tim went back and threw himself completely into his duties at the church. The youth group appeared to be going well. He had around twenty youths in his meetings, and he felt very grateful to have Jessica there to help him with his ministry. Their friendship really blossomed over the next six weeks, but Tim found himself fighting the hidden feelings he had for Jessica.

He tried to justify his reasoning for not allowing himself to express his feelings towards her. Tim thought the congregation might not have fully understood if their youth minister were to begin dating his young assistant. There was also the concern that maybe Jessica didn't feel the same way he did. Tim eventually masked his feelings for Jessica as just a case of simple homesick loneliness. Jessica just happened to be the one that made him feel at home.

During this time together, Tim told Jessica about Charles and Nancy and his concern for Charles's soul. Tim felt deeply touched at the sincerity with which Jessica would listen to him. Even though she was in her early twenties, she listened like a seasoned church counselor.

One cold December, Wednesday night, they sat down in the sanctuary towards the back of the church in one of the pews. The Bible study class had been out for over an hour, and the rest of the congregation had left for the evening. They were the only ones there. These were the moments Tim lived for. He knew she could have left earlier, but she didn't. Despite the fact that the conversation consisted of small talk, it meant the world to Tim.

"Not meaning to change the subject, but when's the last time you spoke to Charles?" Jessica asked.

"Well, it's been about a month and a half now," he answered. "I've been thinking about stopping by and checking on him, especially with Christmas coming up. I can only imagine how hard this holiday will be for him."

"What does your heart tell you to do?" she asked.

"It's telling to me to go see him, or it'll eat at me until I do," he answered back.

"Well, I think you ought to pay him a visit," Jessica suggested.

"Perhaps you're right," he replied with a smile. "I'll go tomorrow afternoon."

"I'll be eager to hear how it goes," Jessica said as she picked up her purse and coat. "Well, I had better be going. It's getting late and colder by the minute outside," she said as they could hear the wind howling outside. "I guess I'll see you Sunday morning."

"Will do," Tim answered. "Again, thanks for listening to me. It really means a lot," Tim said.

Jessica just smiled and made her way out the door.

Tim already missed her and began counting in his head how many days it would be until he could see her again.

CHAPTER 8

Tim stepped out the church front door and flipped up the collar of his black, woolen coat as the cold, north wind hit his face. The snow crunched under his feet as he gasped to catch his breath in the bitter air. He headed down the sidewalk en route to Charles's apartment. Anxiety consumed him on his impending visit. As Tim walked, he rehearsed his lines, but at the same time, he didn't want it to come across as rehearsed. It had been a while since he last spoke to Charles. He hoped this visit would go better than the last one.

He finally reached the apartment building where Charles lived and made his way up the stairs to his flat. Unbuttoning his coat as he went up the stairs, he met a couple of men carrying moving boxes. Tim dismissed it at the time, but to his surprise, the movers were coming from Charles's apartment.

Tim stood in the open doorway and glanced over the boxed-up apartment. As he looked around the room, he heard a familiar voice address him.

"Tim?" asked the voice in a pleasant tone coming from the kitchen area.

"Charles?" Tim responded as he located where the voice originated. "Are you moving?"

"Yeah, looks that way," Charles responded as he stopped to place his hands on his hips, surveying what was left to be packed and moved.

"Where are you going?" Tim asked, almost forgetting that they didn't end on the best of terms when they last spoke.

"Well, actually, I'm going on an expedition in Africa. I'll be working for a scientific researcher," Charles answered.

From the look on Tim's face, Charles anticipated the next set of questions that Tim had on the tip of his tongue.

"I met a researcher from the London University who is a follower of Charles Darwin," he said, looking up to see Tim's mouth drop open at the mention of Charles Darwin, an avid atheist. "He's really helped me see things in a whole new perspective."

Charles looked at Tim with raised eyebrows awaiting Tim's next response.

"You can't be serious, Charles," Tim charged, looking angrily at him.

Charles stared off into the space just past Tim. He exhaled an exhausted breath, as if he was tired of having to explain himself over and over again.

"I've never been more certain of anything else in my whole life," Charles said. "Professor Zen has explained so much to me, Tim. The world is truly a survival of the fittest, and the sooner you realize that, the better off you'll be."

Tim stood in complete shock. The words that were coming out of Charles's mouth caused Tim to go numb all over. Tim suddenly realized that he was losing a friend, and nothing could be done or said that would save him.

Tim felt completely deflated. He knew arguing with Charles would be useless. He stared down at the floor in defeat.

"Tim, why don't you join us?" Charles asked with a sinister smile. Tim broke from his stupor and glared at him. Tim did not appreciate being taunted. Feeling frustrated, he turned and proceeded out the door, leaving Charles alone with his decision.

CHAPTER 9

Over the next couple of months, Tim focused solely on his job. He tried his best to put his friend's new path in the back of his mind, but some days were harder than others. He found support and understanding in confiding his concerns to Jessica. She would often remind Tim of the very same thing that he would preach to his youth group. He tried desperately to mask his feeling for Jessica, but with each meeting he had with her, the more infatuated he became. Tim saw those feelings as a problem instead of a possibility. Jessica and Charles weighed heavily on his mind, each of them being a polar opposite of the other.

"Sometimes you just have to leave you problems with the Lord, and allow Him to take care of it in his own time," she would say to him.

Tim usually felt grateful to hear words of support from Jessica, but this time, he had trouble implementing those words into action.

One afternoon, as Tim made his way back from the grocery market, he began to notice various colored flyers that were posted to light poles and bus stops. Curiosity got the best of him, and he stopped to read one of the flyers. It announced a public viewing of exotic animals recently captured on an African safari for a small admission charge.

Tim felt intrigued to see these animals, but his excitement soon turned to concern when he read that the safari expedition that captured these creatures had been led by Professor Zen, the very man that Charles left to follow. Questions flooded Tim's mind. What on earth would they be doing with these animals?

Just when Tim had started to make headway dealing with Charles's choices, his thoughts were thrust back to it.

The exhibition was set for that afternoon. As Tim went through his daily duties, he tried to weigh the pros and cons of going to it. He checked the clock so frequently that he could swear time had stopped. He had to admit to himself that he felt eager to go to the exhibition, but he questioned whether his excitement was to see the animals or to see Charles. Would he confront Charles or avoid him if he saw him? Either way, he knew he had to go. He couldn't deny it.

A cool breeze from the north fell on the crowd that gathered in the old business district. Many of the businesses along the river had to close when the war started due to the lack of work force available to run the businesses. Outside one of the vacant buildings, a makeshift zoo had been established by Professor Zen's team. The animals on exhibit were impressive for a team of eleven to be able to capture. Among the various creatures, there was a cheetah, a lion, and a very large and alert gorilla.

Tim arrived and almost instantly became caught up in the amazement of the creatures on hand. Never had he had the opportunity to be so close to some of God's true treasures. He wandered along with the crowd as they gazed at each of the animals. When the crowd came to the gorilla, Tim became totally captivated by the beast and found himself locked eye-to-eye with the magnificent creature. He could see the concern in the gorilla's eyes, but it wasn't a look of fear as much as it appeared to be a look of controlled anger. He was totally amazed at how the animal appeared to be so humanlike in his facial expressions and demeanor. As Tim stood there, he was caught off guard by a familiar voice that came from directly behind him.

"Amazing, isn't he?"

Tim turned around to see Charles, but a different Charles than he had last encountered. This Charles looked more rugged. His blond hair was longer and even lighter, and he had grown a beard during his expedition. But along with the beard, Charles seemed to have found his smile and had regained that gleam in his eyes.

"It's good to see you, friend!" Charles said as he came in and gave Tim a big hug.

"Uh," Tim responded surprisingly to the bear hug. "It's good to see you too! It's good to see that smile of yours again!"

"Yeah, it's amazing where you find things. Who would have thought I would have found this smile in Africa," Charles answered.

Tim returned the smile. "Well, it's good to see it." He paused. "Charles, I want to say I'm sorry for—"

Charles put up his hand, gesturing to Tim to stop the apology. "Hey, don't mention it. We were both a little emotional at the time. Water under the bridge."

"Okay…well…tell me what you have been up to?" Tim asked, feeling a little surprised at the sudden forgiveness by Charles.

"Well, as I alluded to, we've been in Africa doing research on these amazing creatures," Charles answered with the confidence of a seasoned salesman. "The creatures truly are amazing. The way that they function in their environment is spectacular."

"And how's that?" Tim asked, wondering where the conversation was heading.

"Why, it's survival of the fittest at its finest!" Charles answered. "These animals opened my eyes to so many things. Everything is so much clearer now. Each one of these animals is the alpha male in each of their groups."

"Alpha male?" Tim asked to make sure he heard his friend correctly.

"Yes, the dominant male in their group dynamic," he replied. "We're trying to determine what it is in each of these animals that make them the alpha male of their species."

Tim decided to sidestep the whole Darwinism topic. He asked, "Oh, so why did you capture them and bring them back to London?"

"Further research, my friend, further research," Charles replied. "We're looking for the missing link."

"Missing link?" Tim asked, realizing that this was not his old friend but someone entirely different from the Charles he had known.

"Yes, the missing link. What gives them the ability to be a superior creature? And how we can find that missing link in us, to find the superior humans?" Charles explained.

"How are you going to do that, Charles?" Tim asked, trying to keep his growing concern masked.

"Oh, you'll see—" Charles began to explain before they were interrupted.

"Charles, are you attempting to recruit an assistant?" asked an impressive man who glowed in confidence.

Tim turned around to see a tall gentleman in black approach them. His commanding walk in his French pin-striped suit caused Tim to feel intimidated. Tim didn't want to admit it, but the forty-something-year-old man appeared to be in tip top shape and very impressive.

"No, Professor," Charles answered, coming to attention as if he were in the military. "He's an old acquaintance of mine"—he paused—"from my previous life."

"Ah, the dark ages," the professor answered with a cocky smirk. "Anyway, Charles, we need to keep moving."

"Yes, sir," he answered as he turned his attention back to Tim. "I'll catch up with you later, Tim," Charles said with a smile and excused himself and went on about his work.

Tim stood there stunned. He couldn't believe the sudden change in the demeanor of his friend. Tim was shocked by his friend's newfound insight of living. Questions about the possession of the animals and the research that Charles and the professor were going to be conducting consumed his mind.

Tim stood there looking at the caged creatures as anger began to swell in him. Tim walked away. Feeling confused and concerned over the plight that his friend seemed to be engulfed in, he just hoped Charles wasn't in so deep that he couldn't get out of it. Either way, Tim needed to find out, whether he wanted to know the answers or not.

CHAPTER 10

Tim found himself wandering about the city for the rest of the day. He tried to convince himself that the research that Professor Zen and Charles were conducting would not be as harmful to the animals as his mind had left him thinking. Feeling distraught, he needed to talk to someone. He wandered the streets until he found himself in a neighborhood that had become slightly familiar. Tim approached an apartment building and walked up the flight of stairs to an apartment door. His heart was beating fast but for reasons he wasn't quite sure of. Tim knocked on the door and waited. He heard the soft footsteps approach the door. The door opened, and he was greeted by a warm, welcoming smile.

"Tim? What brings you by?" asked Jessica.

"Sorry to pop in on you like this, but I really need someone to talk to," Tim responded, "and you're the only one I can really trust."

Jessica opened the door and invited him in. Tim couldn't help the urge to be nosey by giving a quick scan of the apartment. It was cutely decorated with various images of flowers either in pictures or vases, along with candles and lace doilies. It was definitely a young woman's apartment with no signs of a past boyfriend. Tim knew that he had no right to assume her dating status or record, but after all, he was a man, and she was an attractive woman. So naturally, the curiosity was there. He quickly regained focus on the reasons he stopped by.

"What is it?" she asked as they took a seat on the sofa.

"Well, I know you told me that I should just leave my concerns regarding Charles with the Lord, but I ran into Charles down by the river docks in the old business district."

"What happened?"

"He's changed even more. Now he's totally lost," he continued. "They captured these magnificent creatures. I swear, they truly are some of the Lord's finest treasures." He paused to gather his words. "But he told me that they are going to use them for research, and I'm concerned about the experiments they are going to perform."

She reached over and placed her hand on his knee.

"Maybe you should inform the police," she said.

Caught off guard by her gentle gesture, he quickly jumped to his feet and walked over to the window.

"I can't until I know for sure what they're doing," Tim said, knowing that his quick jump from the couch might have hurt her feelings.

He turned around to face her. She sat there looking at him with a concerned and confused look.

"What do you plan on doing, Tim?" she asked.

"I just want to see what they are doing. I'll just take a quick peek. Just enough to confirm if my assumptions are right or not."

"I don't know, Tim. It sounds dangerous."

"I'll be careful, but just in case, I wanted someone to know…you know…just in case," Tim said.

"Please be careful, Tim," she pleaded as she stood up and reached with her arms with intentions of giving him a hug of support. But she quickly brought her hands back up to her chest as if recalling his sudden response to her touching his knee.

She walked him to the door.

Just before he walked out, he stopped and placed his hand on her shoulder and said, "Thanks for being here for me, Jessica. It means the world to me."

Jessica gave Tim a small smile as he closed the door behind him.

A storm began to roll in from the south. The flashing glow from the lightning off in the distance lit up the sky only to be followed by a distantly low, rumbling thunder. Tim had made his way through the dark, abandoned river district where the makeshift zoo had been earlier that day. His heart raced as he looked over the empty buildings, trying to find any hint of activity. He had the guilty feeling of acting like a thief or an intruder as he quietly snuck around the vacant buildings. Finally, right by the river, he found light coming from a glass-enclosed structure attached to a previously occupied warehouse. It appeared to be an old greenhouse. He knew Professor Zen and Charles were conducting their questionable research there.

He made his way down the alley towards the back of the building. As he approached, he could see the light of the room come through the windows and skylights that made up the upper walls and ceiling of the laboratory. Tim studied the makeshift laboratory from the outside. He saw a couple of the windows were open. Slowly he sneaked over to one of the windows where he could hear if any activity was underway inside. Once he positioned himself under one of the windows, he realized why they were open. The stench from the assorted animals flowed out strongly from the opening. Tim had to power through the pungent smell as he strained his ears. He heard what could only be soft growling noises from whatever animal Charles and Zen were working on.

Tim's heart raced. He had to see what was going on. Desperate to look inside, he scanned his surroundings for whatever would assist him. Just then, he located a stack of wooden crates on the vacant shipping dock next to the laboratory. Quickly, he grabbed a couple of the wooden boxes and built a rough structure that would allow him to peer inside. He cautiously climbed the crates, knowing that even a creak of the wood could give his presence away. He finally managed to reach a position where he could to look inside. He scanned the room to find the location of the professor and Charles. He found them both. They were standing over a lab table where they had various vials of fluid lined along the table among the other laboratory equipment.

He scanned over the rest of the lab as a sudden feeling of illness and shock came over him. In the room, the various animals were caged, chained, or strapped against their will. Some of the animals were lying still in their cages, either asleep or dead. Tim felt his heart race as he recognized the magnificent gorilla he had seen earlier that day—the same creature that Tim felt he made some kind of connection with as they looked at each other eye-to-eye. The gorilla was strapped to the lab table. Tim couldn't tell if it was still alive or not. He focused on the animal for a few moments and could finally see the creature breathing. Feeling relieved but acutely aware of the danger in animal appeared to be in. He didn't know the extent of the danger, but he knew these two men had little regard for the well-being of these animals. Their only concern seemed to be obtaining the answers they were seeking by whatever means possible.

Tim watched in horror as he witnessed the professor and Charles approach the gorilla with a large syringe. They drew blood from him as the drugged creature flinched in noticeable pain, even under the heavy sedation. The two then took the fluid and went back to the working lab table and poured it into a metal, cylinder-shaped capsule that appeared to be about ten inches in height. They put other fluids into the container as well. Tim assumed it could only be blood taken from the other animals in the room. They placed the capsule in the laboratory mixer as they both watched intently while the potion mixed together. Tim sat there motionless, feeling the anger and disgust well up inside him. As the anger grew in him, he tried to focus on his next move. That's when it became clear to him to do the only thing he knew he could do, and that was to pray. "Dear, Lord, please help me!" He paused. "Lead me! Guide me! Speak to me! I need to know what to do!"

Then out of nowhere, a bolt of lightning streaked across the sky accompanied by a loud, crackling, popping thunder. Out of complete shock, Tim jumped from his perch, only to lose his balance and come crashing down on the pile of wooden pallets.

Tim's head landed hard on the wooden dock. Knowing the severity of the situation, he tried his best to escape, but his wobbly legs and woozy consciousness gave way to darkness as he saw the silhouettes of two figures rush towards him.

CHAPTER 11

Another loud clap of thunder pierced the black sky over London with enough force that it brought Tim back to consciousness. As his eyes began to clear up, he soon felt the throbbing headache as a result of his previous fall. Glancing around, he found himself lying on a hospital gurney in the middle of Professor Zen's laboratory. Looking up at the skylights, the flash of distant lighting showed the pouring down rain flow down the greenhouse structure.

Checking his surroundings, he located Charles and the professor working at the lab table. They had their backs to Tim as they studied their work. Tim tired to remain calm by praying to himself.

"Dear Lord God Almighty, please deliver me from this situation!"

Tim slowly turned his head to the right and found the mighty gorilla strapped to a gurney next to him. A sudden sense of shock and awe came over him by the creature's sheer presence. He tried to think out his next possible move when he heard Professor Zen bark out orders to Charles.

"Mix the plasmas again," he ordered as he straightened his back and pointed at the laboratory mixer. "And this time, increase the speed."

"Yes, sir," Charles replied as he turned the mixer back on.

Charles glanced over to Tim, but Tim quickly pretended to still be unconscious.

Through squinted eyes, Tim peeked to see the two watch the mixer vigorously spin the capsule that contained the collective plasma shake.

Tim knew he had to stop them, but he wasn't sure if he had enough time to go over a plan completely in his head.

"That's good. Shut it off," ordered Professor Zen as Charles responded by doing exactly as requested.

Charles then took an eyedropper, opened the canister's lid, and took a very small sample of the freshly mixed plasma. He placed a drop on the small glass slide and handed it to the professor.

"Very good, let's have a look," replied the professor as he gestured to Charles that they would use the dual viewer microscope. They put the glass slide in place and began to examine it.

Another bolt of lightning flashed across the sky with the thunder traveling close behind. Neither man flinched. Both men were totally enthralled in the experiment.

Tim saw his chance. He quietly slid off the table and crawled over next to the gorilla. He peered up to where he was nearly face-to-face with the creature. His heart jumped when the gorilla opened its eyes and met his own. An automatic impulse caused Tim to put a finger to his mouth in a gesture to tell the gorilla to be quiet, and to Tim's surprise, he felt the gorilla understood.

Tim carefully began to unbuckle the straps that held the animal down. He prayed that the gorilla wouldn't break loose and cause havoc before he had him freed. He unbuckled the last strap, and the gorilla didn't move in the slightest.

"Go," Tim whispered, waving to the gorilla to attack, but instead, the creature just lay there. He appeared to be heavily sedated and incapable of moving on his own.

Okay, plan B, Tim thought to himself. He began to focus on the capsule that contained the precious plasma of the collective male animals.

He crawled towards the table where the metal container rested. Professor Zen and Charles were on the opposite side of the laboratory, still fixated on what they saw through the microscopes.

Knowing full well that their research depended on whatever chemical that capsule contained, he decided to take it and make a run for it. The gorilla and the other creatures would have to be on their own until the authorities arrived. As he reached up to grab it, he accidently knocked over a row of glass vials. As he listened to the thin glass tubes break, Tim held is breath, waiting for the inevitable.

"What in the world…" the professor yelled as he looked up.

Tim tried to hide behind the table, but he knew he was caught.

"What are you doing?" Zen shouted.

The professor ran over to Tim and grabbed him by the arm.

"Who do you think you are, disturbing my research?"

The professor glared at Charles as if wondering if Charles knew who he could be.

"I think he came by to look at our collection yesterday," Charles answered.

Tim began to realize that Charles was protecting his identity from Professor Zen.

Charles ran over and picked Tim off the floor abruptly like a police officer picking up a drunk of the ground.

"You heard him. What are you doing here?" he asked Tim.

"I think the question is, what are you doing here?" Tim yelled as he cringed in anger and a little discomfort from the manhandling by Charles.

"It's none of your business!" Charles growled as he quickly shook Tim with his grip.

"Charles, it's all right," said Professor Zen as he stood there casually with his hands clasped behind his back.

Zen walked slowly around the laboratory as Tim and Charles stood frozen, anticipating his next move. Charles kept a firm grip on Tim, waiting on his next orders.

"It's all right indeed." He smiled a sinister grin and turned and began to walk away from them.

Charles tightened his grip on Tim's arm. Then with an angry glare, he the mouthed the question, "What are you thinking?"

Tim didn't answer; he just returned the glare. Charles then turned his attention back to Zen.

"What are we going to do with him?" Charles asked.

"He's just a street rat, he won't be missed," Zen coolly responded.

Charles finally looked at Tim with a concerned look.

"How do we know that?" Charles asked.

Tim thought he heard a hint of desperation from Charles to save his former friend.

The professor walked to the dark corner of the lab. Tim had a hard time seeing him. He could hear the latches of a case open and the mechanical clicks and locks of a device.

"We'll have to do our own extermination of the vermin," Professor Zen said smoothly.

Tim watched as the professor eerily emerged back into the light carrying a large rifle. Tim assumed it was the very same rifle Zen used to capture or kill the animals on their African safari. Zen carried the rifle with pride.

Charles released his grip on Tim and dashed to over to Zen's side. Tim stood frozen in fear.

"Can't we just let him go? He won't say anything," Charles responded quickly.

"Sorry, I can't take that chance," the professor said coolly as he took aim at Tim.

Tim felt his heart nearly stop. He couldn't breathe, let alone speak. He just prayed to himself, "Please, God!"

Just then, Charles was attacked and sent sailing across the room. To Tim's amazement, the gorilla had sneaked off the gurney, moved around the dark portions of the laboratory without being seen, and attacked Charles. Then the animal turned his attention on the professor, who stood in shock at seeing the creature freed. The gorilla then swung with his powerful arm and knocked the professor back, slamming him against the table. Tim watched in awe as the gorilla quickly took out the two men and saved him from certain death. The animal then proceeded to walk towards the table, holding the capsule of collective plasma. The creature grabbed the canister as if he knew the importance this container held.

Zen crawled over to his rifle and somehow mustered the strength to aim the rifle and pull the trigger just as the gorilla drew his arm back in attempt to throw the capsule with all his might. The bullet hit the gorilla in the upper left shoulder. The beast roared in pain but kept his position and refocused his glare on Zen. The Professor quickly manned the single slot action rifle and took aim again and fired, striking the gorilla in the abdomen.

The creature staggered back, bending over then straightening itself, and began to approach Zen again. The gorilla pulled his right hand back, holding the canister, and attempted to heave it again. The professor, fearing for his life, quickly manned the rifle again and took one more shot. Then instantaneously, the laboratory became filled with an electrical, blinding light and deafening sound.

The professor had managed to send off the third shot just as a lightning bolt crashed through the laboratory skylights. The bolt of electricity struck the gorilla at the same time as he was hit by the third bullet. The electrical shock caused Tim to black out as the room went dark and fell completely silent, except for the echo of the thunder rumbling throughout the city.

CHAPTER 12

Tim woke up to find himself strapped to a laboratory bed, lying there in nothing but his white boxer briefs. He spent a couple of moments trying to clear his head. The last thing he remembered was seeing the gorilla being shot by Professor Zen at the same moment a lightning bolt had come crashing through the skylights of the lab.

Tim took a quick assessment of his body. The only pain he felt was the residual headache from the evening's events. He slowly looked around the room. Tim could see that tarps had been placed over the hole in the skylights to keep the rain from pouring in. Glancing around the room, he found Professor Zen standing at the laboratory table again, looking through the microscope. Charles stood next to the professor. Charles appeared to be a little wobbly still from the recent events. He noticed that both Charles and the professor had blood on their white aprons. But where did the blood come from? Then he felt a cold rush come over him inside. He looked to his right and saw the gorilla lying on the floor at the same place where he was shot and struck dead.

Tim felt ill. He could tell that the two men had done some sort of procedure on him, but he wasn't certain what they had done. He lay there mourning for the gorilla.

Tim rolled his head back to his left. His eyes met Charles.

"He's awake now, professor," Charles said.

Charles stared at Tim with a blank look.

"What are you doing?" Tim asked as the two of them approached him through the heavily damaged laboratory.

"Well, we've been telling you for some time that it's none of your business," Charles answered. "But now, it's about to become your business."

"It's a funny thing," the professor said. "You do all these experiments, do all this testing, and nothing happens," he said as he turned to meet Tim's eyes with a sinister smile. "Then someone comes along, pokes his nose where it doesn't belong, and attempts to sabotage everything you've been working for! But somehow, instead of creating more problems, it appears the project's problems are now solved," he continued. "And thanks to you, we'll be able to move on to the next phase."

"I don't understand," Tim said. Panic began to set in as he tried to wiggle himself free from the table straps.

"Oh, I know you don't. In fact, I'm not sure myself," the professor replied as he walked around the bed as if giving a lecture to his college class.

"All I know is that, now, the plasma is continuously stirring around inside the capsule on its own. And the temperature is at one hundred one degrees. Very warm for any animal to sustain individually, but together, they are now interacting with each other with this enormous energy." He paused and gave a smile of twisted sincerity. "And I have you and your gorilla friend to thank for that. You see, that bolt of lightning seems to have changed the configuration of the plasma inside."

He stopped to prep Tim's arm with a swab of alcohol.

"Now, we have to start all over with a new subject. Would you do the honors?"

"What are you doing?" Tim asked as his voice began to shake in fear.

"Research," Charles answered coldly, meeting Tim with a cold glare.

"This might sting a bit," the professor said as he injected Tim with a dose of the plasma.

Tim screamed in pain as the professor struck him with the needle hard. He could feel the warm plasma enter his system and felt it run through his veins, reaching his heart. Then, like a mild shock, he felt it being shot out to all the extremities of his body from the heart as it pumped vigorously away.

"There. We'll give it a moment to adhere to your system," the professor said. "Oh, and here's a little memento for you." He pried Tim's right hand open and placed three blood-stained, gold bullets in his hand. "We pulled these out of your friend's dead carcass."

Professor Zen and Charles turned away from Tim and went back to the table. Little did they know that as soon as the professor placed those three gold bullets in Tim's hand, Tim instantly felt a strange sensation come over him. He felt his blood warm, his muscles enlarge, and his face and body stretch, along with an enormous amount of strength that came over him. Then suddenly, Tim felt the explosion of hair cover his entire body.

"Charles, turn on the mixer again. I want to see if it changes the dynamic of the plasma's structure," Professor Zen ordered.

Charles complied and turned on the mixer. The moisture had built up in the laboratory, caused by the lightning bolt that came crashing through the skylight ceiling, allowing rain to come in. Condensation had built up on the mixer, which in turn caused the mixer's motors to whine louder than normal. The whine of the motor was just loud enough to drown out the sound of the straps breaking as Tim's new physique freed him from the table.

"Okay, shut it down," Zen ordered, pointing to the mixer. "Looks like we'll have to put that on our list of new supplies," he said in an agitated tone.

The professor turned around and immediately came face-to-face with a magnificent creature. The creature stood a couple of inches above the professor but would have been taller if he wasn't slightly hunched over. His appearance was half-man, half-gorilla, with long whiskers coming from his upper lip that hung down like an unkempt moustache. The creature was almost completely covered in long, brown hair with streaks of light brown in a lion-like mane around his head and neck.

"Oh my—" was all the professor could to say before the creature backhanded him across his chest, which sent the professor flying back onto the stack of empty crates that once housed their supplies. The professor landed with a thunderous crash, immediately knocked unconscious.

The creature then turned his attention to Charles. Charles stood still, as if frozen solid with fear. The creature walked over to him, and with his left hand, he grabbed Charles's chest and lifted him up by his shirt with incredible ease.

He stared into Charles's eyes and growled, "What have you done?"

The creature could see a red glow of evil in Charles's eyes. A glow that he'd never noticed before.

Lowering Charles down to his feet, the beast then felt the unexplainable urge to place his left hand over Charles's face. He followed his urge and did so and simply said the word that mysteriously came to him: "Repent!"

The beast could feel the evil leave Charles's body and enter his own. Fearful of what had just transpired, the beast tossed Charles across the room like a rag doll. Charles came crashing down on one of the laboratory beds and proceeded to roll off and land on the floor, unconscious.

Seeing the animals still trapped in the cages, the creature knew he had to get help, but how? The beast, consumed with fear now, wondered how he had obtained the ability to drain that evil from Charles. And what would happen to him now? He reached over with his left hand and grabbed the capsule containing the restructured plasma, turned, and ran out of the building. The creature ran, ducking into the alleys and hiding in the shadows. All the while hoping he would find help somewhere.

CHAPTER 13

As the creature ran down the alleys, he could feel the disgusting, acidic bile turn in his stomach. He felt himself start to stumble and become weak and dizzy, all the while trying to hide his monstrous form. He could tell that he had reached a more populated section of the city. Traffic had increased on each street he encountered as he recognized the area as a popular spot for nightclubs and bars. The creature saw people staggering up and down the street as they tried their best to make it to their home after a night on the town.

His vision had become blurry, and his stomach began turning and burning at the same time. In the distance, he saw a female walking in front of the establishments. He could tell by her walk that she was not intoxicated like the other people in the street but appeared to be out of place and seemed to be looking for someone. The creature became fixated on her, knowing that she was out of her element and knowing it would be just a matter of time before someone else recognized it too.

The woman looked up and down the sidewalks, looking in the windows of the pubs, hoping to find the person for whom she searched. A light rain began to come down again, and her desperation and frustration became apparent. A man under a strong spell of alcohol and even a longer spell of not having a bath approached the woman suddenly.

"Are you lost, my love?" asked the drunk with his lit cigarette burning as he talked.

"No," she answered, startled. "I'm looking for someone."

"Aren't we all," he replied as he grabbed her, placing his filthy hands over her mouth, dragging her into the closest alley.

"Now, now," the desperate drunk said. "Just relax, and everything will be fine."

He continued to wrestle her under control.

"First, let's see what we have in your purse," he said as he tried to hold her with one arm while he did his best to open her purse with the other.

Freed of the hand that was covering her mouth, she demanded, "Let me go!"

"Shut up!" he answered. He frantically looked through her bag until he heard someone speak.

"Looks like she wants to be left alone," said the voice from the alley darkness.

"Mind your business, bub!" the drunk yelled as he turned towards the voice, only to be scared stiff when the creature appeared out of the darkness. The beast approached the drunk and began poking his finger repeatedly in the drunk's chest as he spoke.

"This is my business now!" stated the creature as he stared into the drunk's eyes.

The beast went to pick up the drunk, but consumed with the painful burning sensation in his belly, he suddenly bent over and proceeded to vomit.

The creature felt the bile burn as it came up his esophagus and out of his mouth. The drunk staggered backward to find his balance. His cigarette fell out of his mouth and landed in the bile that the creature had just released. Once the cigarette landed on the bile, it ignited it as if it had landed on gasoline. The bile erupted into a purplish flame and hissed like a snake as it burned out.

The drunk stammered back into a wall and found the balance he needed to turn and run out of the alley. The beast instantly felt better inside, and his vision started to clear up. He turned his attention to the would-be victim. She too stood frozen in fear in the presence of the creature. The monster strained to focus on her face and felt surprised to be able to recognize her.

"Jessica?" asked the creature.

Jessica stood there, now even more confused and scared.

All she could come up with was a barely unrecognizable "What?" as she shook in fear.

"Are you okay? And what are you doing here?" the creature asked.

"I'm…I'm…I'm looking for someone," she answered.

"Who are you?" she timidly asked.

"Jessica, it's me, Tim," he answered.

"What?" she said. "But how?"

"I don't know for sure, but I'm scared," the creature said. He paused as he realized that he was still holding the three gold bullets in his right hand that he had been holding since the professor had placed them there. He opened his hand, revealing the bullets to Jessica. He glanced over to the capsule that he had been carrying as well. He had only placed it down before confronting Jessica's would-be attacker. She carefully walked over and gently reached in to take the bullets from his hand.

"Jessica, don't!" he requested. "I don't want this to happen to you."

"Shhh," she said. "Let me help you."

He reluctantly opened his hand, allowing her to take the bullets.

Instantly, the creature started to transform back into Tim. They soon were both aware that Tim was in nothing more than his white boxer briefs. He stood there in embarrassment in front of Jessica, but he was happy to be his old self again. They could hear a crowd starting to gather just outside one of the bars. The would-be drunk assailant took it upon himself to inform the bar of the monster in the alley.

"I think we better get out of here," Jessica said.

Tim quickly nodded in agreement as she took off her coat and gave it to Tim to put on. They both ran down the alley and into the darkness, out of sight.

CHAPTER 14

The rays of the sun came through the window curtains and landed on Tim's face. He felt the warm light, which caused him to wake from his deep sleep. As his eyes focused, he soon realized that he was not in his own bed. He looked around the room, trying to figure out where he could be. Suddenly, he recognized the figure that sat in the corner of the room looking at him.

"Jessica?" he asked.

"Yes, I'm here. How do you feel?" she asked as she got up from the chair and walked over to the couch where he lay.

"Well, other than embarrassed and confused, I guess I'm okay," he answered.

He sat for a moment, trying to recall the events of the previous night. Had it just been a bad dream, or did it really happen? He quickly examined his arms as he lay there. They seemed to be normal and not the hairy, monstrous arms from the night before.

"Did all that really happen?" he asked Jessica.

"Yes," she replied.

"How did I end up here?" he asked.

"We came back here after you saved me in the alley. You came in, and I tried to find some clothes in my closet for you, but by the time I came back, you were sound asleep on the couch," she answered in a very calm voice.

"Oh, Jessica," he replied in embarrassment. "I'm sorry to put you in an awkward situation like this. Please forgive me."

"Tim, there's no need to apologize," she responded, kneeling down beside him and taking hold of his hand.

He felt overcome with emotion. He felt remorse for putting Jessica in this situation where she had to harbor a would-be creature, but at the same time, he was totally captivated by her, and he could feel his heartbeat race as she held his hand.

Then he suddenly realized that he had to be accountable to the church for his whereabouts.

He sat up quickly and said, "I gotta get back to the church!"

He looked around for any clothing that he could wear home.

"It's okay, Tim. I took care of it," she said reassuringly.

Tim looked at her in shock. "How did you take care of it?"

"I told them that you were tending to an old friend that was in a lot of trouble," Jessica explained with a look of hopeful acceptance from Tim.

"What did they say?" he asked.

"They said that they were so glad that they had someone on staff that was willing to give to the needy and desperate," she answered. "I know it's not a complete truth, but I thought that a small lie would be easier to explain than an unbelievable truth."

He smiled and said, "Thank you, Jessica. What would I do without you?"

He breathed a sigh of relief and looked around the apartment for the clock.

"What time is it?" Tim asked.

"It's two-thirty in the afternoon." She paused, looking down, and then looked up at Tim. "It's Thursday."

"Thursday?" he asked in shock. "I've been asleep for two days?"

"Yeah," she said, "but I was able to get a lot done in those two days."

Jessica went on to explain how she spent the past days thinking about what had happened to him. She realized that these events were nothing short than an act of God. Tim didn't go looking for this to happen to him, but for some reason, God had allowed this happen to him. For that reason alone, Jessica knew that she had to convince Tim that this was an opportunity from God, a gift perhaps. Now he had the chance to make a true and monumental difference with it.

During these two days, Jessica went out and found material to make clothing for a cloak for Tim to wear. The material consisted of heavy black wool. The hooded cape would help keep him hidden and yet keep him warm when needed. Even though the material had considerable weight, the strength of the creature could handle it. She then found an old pair of gym sweats, again, black in color. She had cut the sweat pants to make them into shorts, figuring the expandability of the material would benefit Tim in periods of transition. She handed the garments over to Tim. He took them without saying a word. He continued to listen to

Jessica as she explained her actions. Jessica then told Tim how she focused on the three bullets that seemed to be the trigger of Tim's newly acquired power. She thought about the devotion that Tim had for his calling to serve the Lord and His people. She even felt inspired about his conviction to save the animals that the scientists had captured to test for their own gain. Tim truly cared not just for humans, but also for all of God's creatures.

She thought about the coincidence that there were three bullets that contained the special ability to transform Tim. Jessica realized that the bullets represented the Trinity of the Father, the Son, and the Holy Spirit. She knew that she had to do something special with these bullets, to turn them into one special symbol—a symbol that would stand for what Tim would stand for.

"A symbol?" Tim asked.

She stood up, walked over to her desk, and opened a wooden box. Jessica explained how she went to a blacksmith and had the bullets melted and formed into a single shape. Reaching into the box, she pulled out a gold medallion. She turned around and walked over to Tim. Tears were welling up in her eyes.

"I prayed a lot for you over the past couple of days, Tim," she said as her lips quivered. "I prayed for God to heal you. But I realized that I was being selfish for my own wants and needs. I realized that you have dedicated your life to serve God in whatever capacity He wants you to serve in. This is who you are. This is your cross to bear."

She held her arm out and allowed the medallion to fall from the leather straps it was connected to. The gold image dangled in front of Tim's face. He gazed upon the medallion and felt the tears well up in his eyes. Tim sat there speechless as he studied the gold pendant. The medallion was the shape of a *V*.

"Why a *V*?" he asked.

"Well, because you were so vigilant in saving Charles' soul and vigilant about doing the right thing. Regardless of the danger it puts you in, you are determined to put God's creatures before yourself. You're a true vigilante of Lord's treasures."

Standing up, he reached out and took it from Jessica's hand and immediately felt his blood heat up.

His body began to transform. Long, brown hair grew from arms, legs, and chest. He grew an impressive, muscular physique until the transformation caused his arms to hang close to the ground, causing him to hunch over. His nose and jaw stretched down, and a scraggily beard formed on his face followed by the burst of the lion-like mane streaked with dark and light brown.

Tim stood there in his new form when Jessica stepped towards him and embraced him.

"This is your cross to bear. This is your calling. You are VoLt."

CHAPTER 15

Tim moved through the neighborhoods with a brisk walk, just short of an all-out run. His mind and heart raced with anxiety. Would he be questioned by Pastor Canow about his whereabouts over the past two days? He reached the church and ran up the steps and entered through the impressive front doors. Tim entered the sanctuary and looked around for any church staff members. He recognized a couple of regular members that were there doing volunteer duties.

As he stood there trying to catch his breath, he heard a recognizable voice.

"Brother Tim, are you all right?"

Tim turned around to see Pastor Canow standing behind him. The pastor came up the stairs leading from the church basement.

"Yes, sir," Tim answered, putting on a tired smile. "I'm just glad to be home."

"Well, if you don't mind me saying, you look like you've been through a lot," the pastor said as he looked over Tim.

"You have no idea."

"Were you able to help your friend?" the pastor asked.

"Well, only time will tell," Tim answered.

"If you want to talk about it, just let me know," Pastor Canow offered.

"Thank you, sir, but right now, I just need to let the events kind of sink in," Tim replied.

"I understand," the pastor said with a smile.

The pastor patted Tim on the shoulder and walked on towards the front of the church, heading for his office back behind the sanctuary.

Tim breathed a sigh of relief. He felt the anxiety of the encounter start to subside. He knew one day he would tell the pastor the truth, but for now, he knew that that moment would not come anytime soon. Tim proceeded to go on with his normal church duties, all the while trying to analyze all the events that had taken place since he last did his normal routine.

In the pastor's office, Pastor Canow and Tim worked together on the sermon for the next Sunday's service. The pastor seldom asked for assistance on his sermons, but he wanted to direct this sermon more towards the young men and women in the congregation. Naturally, since Tim was the youth minister, the pastor asked for Tim's insight on the issues that seemed to be impacting their lives.

"With our country at war with Germany," Tim stated, "a lot of our young men will be heading for the front lines. They need to know that they are not only fighting for our country but for our God."

"Right." Pastor Canow nodded in agreement, rocking back and forth in his chair. "And until the United States decides to enter the war, our boys will be the only thing keeping us from becoming a Nazi state."

The pastor paused to pull out his notes out of his Bible that quoted scripture that he wanted to use for the sermon. Then a knock came at the office door.

"Come in," the pastor answered.

The door opened, and Carol, the church secretary, popped her head in the door.

"Tim? You have a visitor," Carol said with a concerned look on her face. "He seems rather anxious."

Tim looked over at the pastor as Canow greeted him back with another intrigued look.

"Is this the same friend that you have been tending too?" the pastor asked.

"I don't believe so," Tim answered cautiously. "I don't believe he's well enough to travel this far." Tim got up from his chair. "Thanks, Carol."

He proceeded out the door and headed towards the sanctuary.

As he entered the sanctuary, he couldn't believe his eyes. There, standing in the back by the sanctuary doors, stood Charles. Tim's heart started to race. What did Charles see? What did Charles know? He walked quickly back to Charles. Tim didn't know what he was going to say to him.

As Tim approached Charles, Charles surprised Tim by starting the conversation.

"Tim, first I want to say I'm sorry," Charles started. "I don't know what I was thinking to allow the professor to do that to you."

Tim stood there in disbelief at what he heard. Tim recalled when he consumed the evil that inhabited Charles on the fateful night several days ago. He was not sure how it happened, but nonetheless, glad to see that it did have an effect on Charles.

"I just want to make sure you are okay," Charles said as he stood there with his hands shoved in his pockets as if he was freezing.

"I'm okay," Tim answered, still cautious about Charles's intentions for the visit. "If I may ask, why the sudden change in your position?"

"Well, that's something I want to talk about, if I may," Charles replied.

"What would that be?" Tim again asked cautiously.

"What all do you remember from that night? I mean, how did you…escape?" Charles asked.

"Well, I'm not really sure. I just remembered that I was freed from the straps and ran before I was seen by you two," Tim answered, throwing some guilt back at Charles, letting him know that it was still fresh on his mind.

"What freed you?" Charles asked.

"I don't know. I didn't see what freed me," Tim replied.

"Well, let me tell you, it was a rather impressive creature," Charles said. "It was part gorilla, part man, part…I don't know what. I don't know where he came from. All I know is that he had a profound effect on me. Somehow, he took all this bitterness and anger away from me. I don't know how, but it's truly amazing."

Charles displayed a small smile. It appeared he was reflecting back on his encounter with the creature.

"Well, I'm glad you're seeing thinking clearly now, and I thank you for checking up on me," Tim responded as he attempted to escort Charles out the door. "But if you would excuse me, I've got to get back to work." He gestured with his arm, pointing toward the door.

Charles pulled his hands out of his pockets quickly and held them out in front of his chest, gesturing to Tim to stop.

"Tim, there's something I need to tell you." Tim could see the panic come over Charles's face. "The professor and I had a falling out, if you will. In fact, he tried to kill me," Charles said. Tim looked at him in complete shock.

"What?" Tim uttered.

"He took a couple of shots at me. Luckily for me, he missed."

Tim felt his mouth drop open as Charles continued.

"He remembered meeting you during the animal exhibition, and being told that you and I attended the seminary together." Charles paused. "I'm sorry, Tim, but the professor is obsessed with the plasma formula that we created. He's convinced that you have the plasma and will stop at nothing to get it back. I tried telling him that you don't have it. He kept asking me about you, but I didn't tell him anything."

Charles looked completely drained of energy as he told Tim that he was in danger.

"Just be careful, Tim. He could be anywhere looking for you."

Charles paused for a moment, and then a look of shear panic came over him.

"What is it?" Tim asked.

"I think I know where he might be," Charles said. He turned and started running for the door.

Tim started running after Charles. "Where is he?"

"He's at my church!" he shouted back at Tim.

Charles bolted out the door.

Tim stood there at the top of stairs outside the front door of the church as he watched his old friend frantically make his way through the crowd and across the streets in the direction of the Winchester Church. Tim felt a cold sweat come over him. His stomach turned with anxiety. An internal dilemma began to build. He knew what he had to do, but whose will was this—God's or his own?

CHAPTER 16

Tim ran as fast as he could through the streets of London to reach the Winchester Church, often saying "Excuse me" or "Pardon me" as he dodged or passed pedestrians. Horn blasts also marked his trail as he ignored numerous street laws and darted across various avenues, narrowly missing several automobiles.

Tightly grasping onto his backpack over his right shoulder with his left hand, Tim looked up and saw the church. He scanned the alleys adjacent to the church, hoping to find a way inside undetected.

Upon reaching the side alley on the east side, he found a side door. Biting his lip, he turned the doorknob and found it unlocked. Letting out a heavy breath, he slowly opened the door and crept inside. Advancing up the staircase quietly, he could hear shouting going on inside the sanctuary.

"Get in there! All of you!" a mysterious voice barked.

"Leave them out of this! This doesn't concern them!" shouted another voice.

Tim recognized the voice of Charles as he pleaded for their lives.

Tim slowly moved toward the top stair and peeked into the sanctuary. He found Professor Zen holding a Ruger pistol and pointing it at the small group of hostages, waving it back and forth. He appeared to be directing them to enter a small room just off the sanctuary.

"Please let us go," pleaded an older lady. She shivered in place and covered her face with her hands.

"Pathetic, weak people," Zen said. "Where's your God now? Who has the power now?"

He waved his gun, almost in a taunting manner.

Tim knew the situation was dire. He had to act fast. Quickly, he took off his shirt and threw on the cloak. Reaching his in backpack, he grabbed the medallion and hung it around his neck. The transformation began.

Entering the alley again, he ran with all his might, leaping off the ground and busting through the stained glass window that opened to the very room where Zen held his hostages.

Splinters of glass filled the room as everybody took cover. Landing on all fours, in the middle of the room, the creature rapidly scanned the room until he found the professor.

Zen stared wide eyed at the monster before him.

"You!" Zen shouted.

"Me," the creature answered back.

Zen took aim at him, but the angered beast quickly landed a devastating backhand smack upside the professor's head, sending him sliding across the wood floor collecting numerous pieces of shattered glass. He came to a stop as he hit the wall just below the broken stained glass window. Zen attempted to get up, but he collapsed onto the hard floor unconscious.

Charles slowly walked over to the creature with his hands in front of chest, his palms facing the beast. Then he uttered the question everyone in the room wanted to know.

"Who are you?"

The creature looked around and made eye contact with every one of the twelve previously held hostages. Then he bowed his head and said, "My name is VoLt."

"VoLt?" Charles asked. "What does that mean? Does it stand for something?"

"Vigilante of Lord's treasures."

VoLt looked at the window that he had come crashing through.

"I'm sorry about the window, but…" He paused, leaving the obvious unsaid.

VoLt turned and walked out of the room and into the sanctuary. Feeling the uneasiness within the crowd, he knew it was best to leave as soon as possible.

VoLt turned to Charles and asked, "What did Zen want?"

"Well, he's looking for the formula that we were working on," Charles answered.

The creature saw remorse come over Charles' face. He quickly saw the opportunity to address the issue of animal cruelty instead of discussing the location of the missing formula.

"You better contact the authorities and tell them you have Professor Zen here. Perhaps if you cooperate with them, then maybe," VoLt said, stopping short of telling Charles that his punishment might be lighter for the same crime.

"You're right, at least I didn't attempt to kill anybody," Charles responded.

VoLt walked toward the darkened stair case that he originally watched Zen hold the church members hostage, all the while being followed by Charles. Stopping and turning around, he looked at Charles.

"You better tend to your congregation. Make sure they're all right," VoLt suggested.

Charles turned around and looked toward the direction of his church members.

"Perhaps you're right, and besides, I better call the authorities and have them pick up Professor Zen. But if I may ask, how do we contact you if we need your assistance again?"

As Charles continued to talk, VoLt quickly disappeared out of sight and into the staircase unseen. Once he made it down the staircase, he quickly located a small room in the basement where he could transform back into Tim.

Knowing he had to protect his new alter ego and yet show his support for his friend, he knew he had to show up as himself as well. Finding another exit on the west side, he quickly ran out only to run back to the front and through the main doors of the church.

Tim ran inside, finding Charles speaking to other church members.

"Charles, is everything all right?" Tim asked.

"Yeah, thank goodness," Charles answered. "You wouldn't believe it. That creature, VoLt, he showed up out of nowhere!"

"Really?" Tim responded.

"Yeah, saved the day, you could say. He stopped Zen before anybody was hurt."

"Where is Zen?" Tim asked.

"He's in here," Charles answered.

Tim followed Charles into the room where Zen lay unconscious, but a cold chill ran down Tim's spine when both he and Charles discovered that Professor Zen had vanished.

"What? I don't believe it! He was right here just a moment ago!" Charles yelled.

Tim didn't say anything. He just scanned the room, trying to see how and where the professor managed to escape. Tim walked over to the broken window and saw several shards of broken glass in the alleyway, almost leaving a small path in the direction that Zen had made his getaway.

Tim brought his head back inside and looked at a depleted Charles.

"Well, this can't be good."

CHAPTER 17

In the days following the Winchester Church incident, Tim realized that Charles was making an honest attempt to rebuild their friendship. He would stop by on occasion at the Berthel Church to visit with Tim. On one of the earlier visits, Charles told Tim that members of the church had agreed to keep the incident quiet. Some wanted to keep quiet out of fear of Professor Zen while others wanted to protect the vigilante that came in and saved them. Tim could see that Charles was still riddled with guilt over all of his actions as an understudy of Professor Zen.

Charles surprised Tim on occasion by attending Sunday service a couple of times at the Berthel Church. Charles's presence pleased Tim, but it also caused some careful maneuvering on Tim's part as he tried to keep both Jessica and Charles away from each other.

Tim tried his best to express his concern to Jessica for keeping the two apart. Tim witnessed firsthand the heartbreak that Charles went through and the fall that ensued. He wanted to protect Charles and help him to recover. He knew that if Charles ever discovered his budding relationship with Jessica that it might just turn Charles into a downward tailspin. Tim didn't want to take that risk. He just wasn't sure if Jessica fully understood.

In Tim's conversations with Charles, the topic of Charles turning himself in would often come up. But Tim suggested to Charles that perhaps he should lay low and not turn himself in to the authorities. Both agreed that they should wait until Zen was found and arrested to make sure that Charles would not be held solely responsible for their actions.

On a Sunday, one month after the Winchester Church incident, Tim and Charles made plans to meet at a café for a late lunch. It happened to be the same café where Tim met Charles and Nancy for dinner on the night when the German air raid took Nancy's life. Charles insisted on eating there as a step of recovery that he had never allowed himself to have.

As Tim prepared to leave for the café, he decided to change into some casual clothes instead of his normal church attire. He didn't want to give Charles the feeling that he was still "on the clock." As he made his way through the nearly vacant sanctuary, he felt that he was being watched. He looked over at the left-hand side of the sanctuary and recognized the figure watching him. It was Jessica, sitting in her regular spot. She sat there alone, her hands holding a small, gold locket and rubbing it back and forth with her thumbs nervously.

Tim felt a tug at his heart and walked over to her.

"Hi, Jessica," he said.

"Hi," she replied with a small voice as she focused on her hands.

He walked over to the pew she sat in and stood beside her.

"Is there something wrong?" he asked cautiously.

"That's funny. I was going to ask you the same thing," she said, refusing to look up.

"You've barely spoken to me for two weeks now," she said as her voice started to crack.

Guilt consumed Tim.

"I'm so sorry, Jessica," he said. He swallowed hard, and he attempted to explain himself.

He entered the pew just in front of hers. He sat down and turned to his side to face her, realizing that it might look more like a counseling moment as opposed to a lover's spat to any onlookers. She looked up at him and slightly rolled her eyes at him, as if this subtle act by Tim confirmed her fears that he thought they were getting too close. Tim realized what she felt and reached over and placed his hand on hers in an attempt to calm her fears.

"Please allow me to explain," he asked.

Jessica's expressions indicated that she hated that she allowed herself to show her vulnerability like this. She wanted the truth but not a pity display of affection from Tim.

"Okay then, I'm ready," she said as she looked Tim directly in the eyes, displaying a small, steady stream of tears. Wiping her tears away, she gave Tim her undivided attention.

"Oh," Tim started as he tried to get a handle on the situation. "I know I've been kind of caught up with rebuilding things with Charles. I can't really explain why right now, but I'm supposed to meet him for a late lunch."

She looked at him as if wondering why she couldn't join them yet wondering why Tim would want to spend so much time with someone who literally had tried to kill him.

"Well, I'll be eager to hear how you luncheon goes," she said with a raised eyebrow.

Tim responded by bobbing his head up and down in agreement with her.

"Would it be okay if I stopped by afterwards to talk?" he asked.

"I guess that would be fine," she said as she tried to regain her composure. "What time can I expect you?" she asked.

"How about seven?"

"Seven will be fine," she replied with a blank look, letting him know that he was not off the hook just yet. She gave him a small wave, excusing him to leave to meet with Charles.

Tim took the cue and headed out of the church toward the café.

As he walked to the café, he felt his stomach turn. The last thing he wanted was to hurt Jessica. Tim wanted to tell her how much she meant to him, but at the same time, he wondered where this new path was taking him. In his heart, he knew he had to save Charles's soul. After all, that is the main reason he volunteered for this position, to help save souls. But the newly acquired abilities had him questioning nearly everything.

Hopefully later tonight, he'll find a way to repair any and all damages with Jessica, and maybe discover a way to bring the three of them together. It would be one less secret to keep.

CHAPTER 18

A light rain fell down on the streets as Tim walked hurriedly through the neighborhoods to reach the café where he was supposed to meet Charles. Tim felt a little uneasy about meeting there, but Charles insisted.

Tim reached the café and felt surprised at how busy the restaurant appeared to be. He walked in and glanced around the room. An empty table could not be found. He gazed back and forth until he saw Charles waving halfway to the back along the right wall of the restaurant. Tim felt glad to see the smile on Charles's face as they made eye contact. Tim quickly recalled the last couple of months that the two of them had gone through, feeling amazed that they were back to being friends. He made his way around the tables and the other patrons until he reached the pub table where Charles sat.

"I was beginning to wonder if you were going to stand me up or something," Charles said with a smile as he leaned over and slapped Tim on the shoulder as he sat down.

"Yeah, sorry about that. I got caught up with some business as I was leaving," Tim responded. He felt guilty inside for not being able to tell Charles about Jessica. He knew that Charles might not take the news well with Nancy's death still fresh in the months that had followed.

"No problem, man," Charles answered with an understanding smirk.

They sat there for the next two hours. They ate and reminisced about the good old days at the seminary. Even the moments that recalled Nancy were met with fondness and laughter. As the crowd diminished, the volume of their voices didn't, until Tim noticed that his laughter echoed throughout the café.

"Wow, looks like we ran off the crowd," Tim said as he surveyed the nearly empty café.

He glanced down at his watch. He couldn't believe how quickly the time had flown.

"Which reminds me. I need to be taking off here soon."

"Where are you off to? Got a hot date or something?" Charles asked.

"Yeah, something like that," Tim responded with a sarcastic smirk.

Charles laughed heartily in response.

As Tim grabbed for his jacket, he asked Charles, "So what about you? What are you going to do?"

"Aww…I'll probably hang around here for a bit. There's an apple pie over there with my name on it. That was Nancy's favorite dessert. Apple pie a la mode." Charles answered as he looked over where the pies sat on the register counter.

"Sounds good." Tim said.

Tim patted and squeezed him on the shoulder, "I'll catch up with you later."

"Sounds good," Charles responded, and with that, Tim made his way across the café and headed out the door.

Tim had made it about two blocks when he turned around. He made sure he was out of sight of the café, but more importantly, he wanted to make sure he was no longer in Charles's sight. Once he knew the coast was clear, he crossed the street, ran across the next block, and headed back north in the same direction he had just come from. He hated keeping a secret from Charles and hated having to hide his relationship with Jessica from everybody else. Just hearing the word *relationship* run through his mind overwhelmed him. He dedicated his life to God in serving Him and just assumed that love and marriage would not be in the plans for him, but after the events of the past month, he had no idea what the plans God had for him were going to be.

He continued down the sidewalk towards Jessica's flat. The anticipation grew in him. Even though he had been spending a lot of time with Charles as of late, Jessica had always been on his mind. The closer he got to her apartment, the faster he realized he moved. A light sprinkle continued to fall on the city as the evening came on. He finally reached her apartment building and double-stepped the stairs to her flat. He tried to calm his racing heart and breathe before he knocked, but he couldn't wait another moment to see her. His heart raced more as he could hear her walk across the floor after he tapped on the door. She opened the door, looking at him with her big, puppy-dog, green eyes. He could feel his heart melt.

He smiled at her and said, "You know, I've kind of missed you."

She smiled back and embraced him with a huge hug.

Tim spent most of the evening catching Jessica up on his progress with Charles. He truly felt that he had been doing what he was called on to do—saving Charles's soul.

Jessica apologized as she explained how she felt jealous of the time Tim spent with Charles.

"This is new to me too. I've never been this close to someone before," Jessica said.

"I know, me too," Tim responded.

Finally, they were making known to each other the possible mutual feelings they were having.

"Okay," she said with a humble smile, "I guess I can let you off the hook."

She continued smiling as she got up from the couch. As she passed Tim, who sat on the other side of the couch, she playfully ran her fingers through Tim's light-brown hair. Then she walked over to the kitchen to pour another cup of tea for them. Tim sat still as goose bumps ran down his spine as his body enjoyed the tingling sensation of her gentle touch.

"So, what have you been up too?" he asked as he stood up to meet her halfway across the kitchenette to get his cup of tea.

"Oh, not much," she said. "I've been trying to—"

She stopped mid sentence as an interruption came in—a haunting hum from outside. She looked at Tim. He could hear it too. It didn't take Tim long to recognize the noise that caused him to feel ill inside as well as nervous—another Nazi air raid. As soon as they peered out the window, the air raid sirens started to wail.

"Better get our coats," Tim politely ordered as they grabbed the coats and headed downstairs toward the building's basement.

As they opened the doors, other tenants and their families were already running down the hall. Tim couldn't help but notice how some people acted as they filed into the staircase. Some of the neighbors reacted as if they were simply going to retrieve a newspaper. Others appeared to be annoyed, while others looked genuinely concerned and scared. Then Tim saw a man and woman trying to comfort their three small children ranging in ages from three to seven. He felt sympathy for the parents as they tried to console them, and yet he felt an anger form in his belly. It appeared to be a different anger that he normally felt toward the Nazis; this seemed to be an anger that was demanding action. He felt this anger bubble a couple of times recently and knew exactly when and how it resonated. He felt himself take some deep breaths as he calmed the beast inside him.

As they reached the basement door, Tim stopped and waited for the tenants to get inside. Being a guest to the building, he didn't feel right taking someone else's spot. Jessica stood by him, even received a couple smiles of approval from her female neighbors on her new friend amid the chaos that was going on outside. They stood in silence as they heard the bombs whining in the air. They all held their breaths as they waited for the bombs to land. Then the sickening boom could be felt, soon followed by another, then another.

"They seem to be hitting about five to ten blocks from here," said an older tenant of the building as he peered out the basement window.

Tim eased toward the front door of the building to assess the situation. The gentleman was right. They appeared to be in the clear for tonight. He scanned the skies just above the rooftops. A faint, orange glow could be seen coming from the direction where it appeared that the bombs had struck.

In the distance, the sound of sirens could be heard approaching the burning buildings. The anger grew in Tim. Jessica gently placed her hand on Tim's forearm as they stared at the orange glow rising from the rooftops just blocks away. He glanced at her hand on his arm and then turned to look her in the eyes.

"Hey…" he started but found himself unable to finish the sentence.

"I know," Jessica replied.

Tim grabbed her, and they embraced.

"Be careful," she said as she held back tears.

He didn't say anything; he pulled himself away from her and walked out the door and began running down the sidewalk toward the Berthel Church.

Nobody seemed to pay him much attention as he made his way through the crowds of people that were coming out of their shelters. They were all fixated on the glow that lit up the night sky.

CHAPTER 19

The heat coming from the building was much more intense than VoLt had expected. He stood silently on the rooftop as he looked across the alley at the burning structure. He strained to hear any signs of life inside. Then, above all the sirens and crackling flames, he could hear the cries for help inside the inferno.

Taking a deep breath, VoLt charged toward the building. Just as he reached the edge of the rooftop, he leaped in the air, sailing smoothly over the alley. He then tucked himself into a huge ball and smashed into a glass window of the burning structure.

He crashed through the window as shattered glass covered the vacant room. VoLt kept the somersault position as he hit the floor and continued to roll over once and then opened his stance and landed on his feet as if he had performed this maneuver on more than one occasion.

VoLt scanned the room for trapped tenants. The flames had reached the corners of the room from the floors below. The smoke started getting thicker by the second. He spun around and studied the closed door in front of him. He strained to hear anyone on the other side of the door.

He reached out and felt the door, discovering it wasn't hot. Without trying the doorknob, he threw his shoulder into the door with such force that it opened with a loud bang. The sudden noise caused a scared scream from someone in the room. VoLt cautiously entered the room and saw the shadowed outline of three individuals huddled in the corner. As he walked closer, they shouted in horror as the creature approached him.

VoLt quickly raised his hands with his palms facing out.

"I mean you no harm!" he growled over the crackling flames echoing through the building. "I'm here to help!"

As he approached the huddled family, he found a father, a mother, and their daughter. He knelt down in front of them as they continued to look at him in horror and disbelief.

"We have to move now! We don't have much time!" he growled again.

He reached out his hand to help whoever trusted him. To his surprise, the young daughter reached for him without hesitation.

"Lizzy!" shouted the father as he watched the creature take his little girl and vanish into the smoke.

As VoLt readied the girl for escape, he turned slightly to see the mother and father crawl to the doorway. Bracing the girl in his arms, he ran across the floor and leaped out the window. As he sailed through the air, he extended his right arm and grabbed the steel railing of the fire escape of the adjacent building. Caught off guard by his momentum, VoLt hit the wall of the building with his back. Absorbing the brunt of the stop with his back, he managed to protect the young girl from any injury.

Grimacing slightly, he placed the daughter on the fire escape steps. Turning and grabbing a window frame, VoLt easily popped it open to safety.

But the daughter insisted on staying there on the fire escape until her parents were safe.

VoLt then turned around and leaped back inside the burning room. The flames were growing more and more intense. He walked over and, without asking, grabbed the mother, cradled her in his arms, and again ran and leaped out the window, landing safely again on the fire escape. As he sat the mother down next to her daughter, a larger roar came from the building. It had begun to collapse on the front side of the building. The mother screamed in horror, realizing that her husband might not survive.

VoLt stood there for a moment as he surveyed the burning building.

He looked at both of the women and growled, "Stay right here! We'll be right back!"

He climbed on the railing of the fire escape where he had placed the two survivors then leaped across the alley and caught the bottom window sill with his hands as his body slammed into the brick wall, which had begun to weaken from the heat of the fire. VoLt could feel some of the bricks budge in as he hit the wall. Luckily, it held, and VoLt managed to pull himself up and reenter the room where he had left the father. He could see the man lying on the floor and realized that the man appeared to be unconscious from all the smoke inhalation. VoLt knew he did not have much time.

He knelt down and picked up the man and threw him over his shoulder. The crackling and popping of the building structure started to grow louder and louder. He could feel the flooring underneath his feet start to sway and give. VoLt then began running for the window. They were just footsteps away from escape when the floor finally gave way as flames started bursting through. VoLt managed to leap just as the floor disintegrated underneath his feet.

VoLt came flying out of the window through the flames that now engulfed the room. He soared across the alley with the father thrown over his right shoulder. Reaching out with his left arm, he grabbed the railing of the fire escape. His body landed hard against the structure, but he managed to take the brunt of the impact in order to protect the father. The mother and daughter watched as their family member had been miraculously rescued. The mother and daughter nervously screamed as the frame shook violently. Once the structure had stabilized, VoLt climbed onto the platform where the women were. He carefully laid the man down and checked his breathing. Still breathing, he began coughing once his body recognized clear air.

"He should be okay, but get him some medical attention quick," VoLt said as he knelt down by the man.

"How can we thank you?" asked the wife as he knelt down beside her husband and VoLt, reaching out and placing her hand on VoLt's hand.

"You don't need to," VoLt answered as he reached down and picked up the man and carried him inside. The mother and daughter followed. As they both knelt down to tend to him, VoLt seized the opportunity vanish out of sight.

CHAPTER 20

The quietness of the neighborhood that VoLt crept through was in sharp contrast to the scene from which he had just been. He kept himself hidden in the shadows of the buildings around him. As he stopped to catch his breath, VoLt became aware of a certain perfume that began to fill the air around him. Recognizing the scent, he looked down the street as saw a figure quickly approaching his location. Suddenly aware that his sensory of smell had obviously become enhanced with his new capabilities, VoLt called out to the individual.

"Jessica, over here," said a low, growling voice.

Jessica walked over in the direction of the voice as VoLt stepped out of a boarded-up doorway behind a dumpster.

"Are you okay?" she asked as she reached out to touch him.

"Yes," he answered as he reached up and took off the medallion and placed it in Jessica's hand, which began his transformation back into Tim.

Jessica placed the golden *V* in her coat pocket, and then they embraced each other tightly. Neither one said anything, nor did they need to say anything. They were just grateful to be safe and together.

The chimes from Big Ben echoed over London. It was the only sound that could be heard. The haunting chimes reminded Tim of the events of the evening. He realized that after each Nazi air raid, Big Ben would still be standing and chiming away. Tim always felt that was England's way of saying that they were still there and still fighting. Jessica and Tim walked hand in hand as he walked her home.

"Think you'll be able to sleep tonight?" Jessica asked with a smile in an attempt to lighten the mood.

"Boy, I hope so," Tim answered as he continued looking down at the ground as they walked. "I'm kind of tired."

He looked up and realized that they were back at Jessica apartment building.

"Well, I better let you go," Tim said as he looked up at her window. "I'm sure you're pretty tired too."

Jessica swiveled back and forth, standing in front of him, and lightly grabbed his coat at his chest with both hands and said, "Well, it has been a pretty eventful evening." She leaned in closely and said, "You sure know how to show a girl a good time."

She kissed him softly on the cheek. Then she leaned back and smiled. "See you later?"

"You can count on it!" he said as he returned the smile. She headed up the stairs and went inside.

Tim waited until she was in her flat. She came to the window and gave him a wave, letting him know that she had made it in okay. He waved back and headed back to his quarters. On the way home, he relived the events of the evening, but the thought of Jessica kept putting a smile on his face.

Tim approached home and looked up at the Berthel Church. At night, the church appeared to be eerie yet warm in appearance. The few sources of light inside the sanctuary gave the stained-glass windows a soft glow that at times could be hard to see. Tim walked up the steps and inside the sanctuary. At all hours of the day, members and guests could be found there praying or meditating. Tim had grown used to seeing that, even if it was 1:25 in the morning. He quietly passed the silent people scattered randomly among the pews and walked on to his quarters.

His mind and body were finally calm as he went to open the door of his room, but to his surprise, he found his door ajar. He slowly pushed the door open and felt shocked to see that his room had been ransacked, his bed turned over, sheets and bed coverings strung everywhere. The drawers in his desk were emptied as well as the drawers of his dresser. What Tim noticed almost immediately was that the dresser had been pushed aside to reveal the secret door. Only recently had he hid the canister along with his hooded cloak inside the hidden door and covered it with the dresser.

He quickly realized that the metal canister that contained the plasma was missing.

A cold shiver ran down Tim's spine, and then he broke out into a sweat. Panic raced through his veins. He looked around the room for any evidence of who might have done it.

Could Professor Zen have found him? According to Charles, Zen never discovered his real name. He stood frozen as he tried to determine his next move. Tim quickly decided to put his room back in order before any of the staff members found out. As he worked, he could only think of one person that could help. He just couldn't believe he would be seeing Jessica again tonight, but this time, the situation was dire.

CHAPTER 21

Tim's heart raced as he made his way back to Jessica's apartment. This time, though, it raced out of fear and not excitement. Reaching her building, he double-stepped up the concrete stairs and entered. He tried his best to run up the flights of stairs quietly, but Tim's heavy breathing seemed to be louder than his footsteps.

Reaching her flat, he knocked with three quick taps. Holding his breath, he counted to five in his head and repeated his knock.

Finally, Tim could hear feet make their way to the door.

"Who is it?" Jessica asked through the door.

"It's me, Tim," he replied. "Something's happened," he said just loud enough for her to hear through the door-frame cracks.

She opened the door and quickly allowed Tim in.

"I'm sorry to bother you so late," Tim said.

He quickly stepped inside, shutting the door behind him. Tim didn't want any neighbors to see him at Jessica's apartment so late at night.

"What happened?" she quickly asked as soon as the door closed. "Are you all right?"

"Short answer…no," he answered in an almost sarcastic tone. "Somebody broke into my room and found something."

"You mean the formula?" she frightfully asked.

"Yeah," Tim replied with a hard sigh. "I'm not sure who took it. I don't think it could be Zen. Charles swore that all Zen knew about me was that I was a former friend of his at the time."

He looked over at Jessica. She was standing there with a stunned look on her face.

"Jessica, what's wrong?" he asked.

"Tonight, at the fire, I saw Charles," Jessica explained. "I didn't say anything to him because he didn't seem to see me, and plus, I was eager to meet up with you."

She paced the floor.

"Do you think he saw us?" she asked him.

Tim suddenly felt ill to his stomach. "If he did, then we're in trouble."

CHAPTER 22

The next couple of days were long for Tim. As he trudged through his daily routine at the church, he found himself filled with anxiety. He kept hoping and praying that Charles would stop by or call, but he heard nothing. He felt nauseous at the thought of Charles finding the hidden plasma in his quarters. What would Charles do with it? Even Tim didn't quite understand how it all worked. He just knew that somehow God intervened into their experiment and VoLt was the result.

Charles didn't come to church either that following Sunday, which only fueled Tim's concerns. The next morning, Tim found himself walking down the sidewalk toward Charles's residence. The morning fog still lay heavy at his feet while his heart raced with each step. He reached the old rundown apartment building and stepped into the foyer. He glanced over at the mailboxes at the list of tenants. As Tim scrolled down, he noticed that Charles's name had been scratched off.

Charles only recently rented the small flat in the dilapidated part of the city after he escaped from Professor Zen. Being low on funds, and trying to stay out of sight from Zen and the authorities, it seemed to be a safe location for him.

He jogged up the stairs and knocked on Charles's door. He waited a few seconds and knocked again. He could hear his knock echo through the apartment. Tim attempted to open the door and to his surprise, he found it unlocked.

He slowly cracked it opened and said, "Charles, you home?"

Dead silence. Tim walked inside and found the apartment virtually empty. Trash was strung about. He walked over to the window and looked outside. Guilt rushed through his mind as Tim began to worry about his friend.

"Charles, where are you?" he asked himself quietly.

The sun continued to be hidden by clouds, leaving Tim's modest living quarters dark and cold. Already awake and dressed for the day when others were still asleep, he strapped on his watch and grabbed his keys. His stare fixated on the dresser that hid the secret door. Tim left his quarters and headed toward the sanctuary. He decided to get a breath of cool, fresh air and stepped outside the church doors. Standing on the wide, front step, he watched the movement of the people coming and going. He couldn't help but notice that a larger crowd than normal stood around the newspaper stand. As he watched their body language and descriptive hand gestures, he could tell that something out of the ordinary had occurred. Curiosity got the best of Tim, and he soon found himself digging for change in his pocket to buy a *London Times*.

As he approached the stand, he strained to hear what the people were talking about.

"I wonder if it's the same creature from the other night at the apartment building fire off of Rochester?" asked a gentleman to another.

Tim felt a lump in his throat as he purchased a paper.

He heard another voice ask, "I heard about a sighting in an alley by a bar down at the docks a couple of months back."

Tim's heart began to race. He quickly ran across the street and up the stairs to the church. He entered through the large doors and sat down at the first pew he came to.

The headline instantly caused a headache to form as the words began to sink in. "Three Banks Robbed Overnight At The Hands Of An Unknown Creature!"

His hands turned cold as Tim read about the banks being broken into and robbed of thousands. The story had witnesses describing a tall, hairy, monstrous creature being seen leaving the scene with large bags of money. The creature appeared to be quite strong and agile. Other witnesses recounted the possible connection between this incident and the incident where a family was rescued by a similar creature. The story also reported that Scotland Yard was on full alert and was currently investigating all leads. Tim suddenly felt nervous as he looked up from the paper and looked around to see if anyone had been watching. He stood up and folded the paper under his arm and proceeded to his quarters.

Tim could only think of one thing to do—pray for guidance. He realized that he hadn't prayed much to God about it much lately. He had just assumed that things would fall into place and that God would show him what he needed to do with this newly acquired capability. Now things were falling apart right before his eyes. He knew that Charles had to be behind this new creature that had been breaking into the banks. He didn't have any evidence to prove it, but in his gut, he knew it had to be Charles.

Tim entered his quarters and locked the door behind him. Walking to his bed and kneeling, he quickly bowed down with his hands firmly clasped together and his elbows resting on the bed.

"Dear heavenly Father, please forgive me for my sins. I need your guidance, Lord. I fear Charles has fallen away again, and this time, I fear for his life." Tears began to well up in Tim's eyes as his emotions began to come out. "Please give me guidance to help him."

Tim sat quietly in prayer as he eagerly waited to hear God speak to his heart. As he sat there meditating, there was a knock at the door.

He paused and softly spoke, "Thank you, Lord, amen."

He stood up and walked over to the door. Without saying a word he opened it slightly to see who it could be. It was Jessica, looking very concerned as she held the same paper in her hands.

"It wasn't me," Tim said with a confused look as he responded to the questionable look he was getting from her.

"Well, I didn't think so," she replied, "but do you know who did?"

"I have a good idea," he stopped to glance back at his dresser. "Looks like I'll be working late tonight."

CHAPTER 23

Stars populated the sky as VoLt stood on the rooftop in an older business district of the city. Throughout the evening, he had made the rounds to other banks to ensure that the police were watching for another night of bank robberies. VoLt had happened to notice that this particular part of the city had gone unwatched. Knowing there had to be roughly six banks in this area, he figured he would at least stand guard over this portion of the grid. Just in case.

This was the first time as VoLt that he had time to reflect on his new calling as the creature. The absurdity of it all ran through his mind. After all, he thought he was already doing God's will by serving in the church, leading others to Christ. But now this? It just seemed to be a bit beyond the call of duty. All he knew for sure was that he felt truly grateful to have Jessica in his life to help it all make sense to him.

As his mind wandered, a distant blast broke his trance. Turning his attention in that direction, VoLt figured it to be about three blocks away. Attributing his enhanced hearing to one of his many new powers, he was certain the blast was fairly small. But realizing there wasn't anything normal behind it, he went to investigate.

Moments later, VoLt stared down at the back entrance to the Premium Bank. Remnants of the blast cloud still lingered in the air. VoLt felt his mood change as he quickly scaled down the building and approached the bank's back door.

VoLt quickly crept in as he could hear someone frantically break into the teller's cash drawers.

A quick sense of relief came over him as he realized that it wasn't Charles or the creature that had been reported on in the newspaper. It appeared to be just a common thief.

VoLt listened as the robber seemed to be reciting instructions out loud to himself.

"Just get the cash in the cashier's drawers. Don't worry about the safe," the thief said.

VoLt watched almost in amusement at the robber's antics. The thief pried the cash drawer with a crowbar. The drawer popped violently open and shot out from the counter, sending the cash contents all over the small confines of the cashier's post.

"Great," the thief said.

The robber picked up what cash he could see with the help of the streetlights shining through the windows.

"Expecting more?" VoLt growled.

VoLt emerged from the darkness, knowing his sheer presence would be enough to scare the thief.

"What in the world?" the robber yelled.

He dropped what cash he had in hand as he stammered back into the clerks' counter.

VoLt approached him and picked him up by the shirt and brought him up to his face. "Are you the one responsible for last night's robberies?" VoLt growled.

"Uh…no way! It wasn't me!" the man answered.

VoLt could hear the sirens approaching in the distance, and knew his time was limited. VoLt looked at the grimy man and could see the light-red glow in his eyes.

He placed his hand over the thief's face and said, "Repent!"

VoLt could feel the hot sin exit the thief's body and mysteriously enter his own. VoLt felt the bile form in his stomach. It began to turn hot and started to burn. VoLt dropped him from his hold. The thief fell like a sack of rocks. Stepping out into the alley, VoLt turned his head and spewed the vomit out of his mouth. The yellowish-green liquid landed on the ground and sizzled as it lay there. VoLt took a match, lit it, and dropped the burning match onto the center of the waste. It caused it to ignite in a quick, purple flash as it hissed into evaporation.

Reentering the bank, VoLt turned his attention back on the thief and asked, "Who put you up to this?"

The man appeared to be surprisingly calm as he smoothly answered. "He just simply told me that if anyone asked"—he paused—"I was to tell them that Evilution sent me."

VoLt stood silently as he looked out the window at the flashing police cars approaching. The robber also stood and glanced out the window. VoLt took the opportunity to exit as he listened to the thief mumble to himself.

"Well, I guess the jig is up, as they say."

VoLt stood on the edge of an adjacent building overlooking the arrest of the thief. He could still taste the vomit in his mouth. Clearing his throat and spitting the last bit of the remnants of the cleansing, he watched them put the thief in the squad car and drive off.

VoLt scanned the other nearby rooftops, but there was no sign of the thief's employer. He knew the man to be nothing more than a calling card. His head began to throb as he began to realize that somehow, Charles was this creature that called himself Evilution.

How did Charles achieve this? The name itself, "Evilution," was nothing more than a verbal slap in the face, a slam on Tim's own beliefs and religion. The sure anger and evil that resonates in that name must be a window to the soul of the creature itself.

Other aspects began in seep in VoLt's mind. How did Charles gain access to plastic explosives. One would have to know contacts and have a good-sized bank roll to obtain material like that. His stomach turned as the pieces began to come together in his head. Charles appeared not to be working alone. The only person that Charles knew that had access to that type of material would have been Zen. If by some chance Evilution had made an alliance with Professor Zen, then there's no telling what the two had planned.

VoLt, feeling on the disadvantage, knew that he had better change his strategy from a defensive mindset to that of an offensive one. He would have to rely on all aspects of his newly acquired abilities in order to overcome his adversaries.

CHAPTER 24

The pinging alarm of his clock went off early for someone who didn't get to sleep until three o'clock in the morning. Tim reached over to silence the ringing. He lay there on his stomach as he stared at the clock. It was 7:30 a.m., and Tim did the math in his head—only four and half hours of sleep. Not nearly enough to keep up with the pace he had been going. Slowly, he got up and dressed for the day. His revelation from the previous night constantly filled his mind.

As the day went on, Tim's anxiety level continued to rise. It was Wednesday, which meant youth Bible study tonight. Like clockwork, Jessica showed up at 6:40 to help with the group as she had since Tim began his service at the church. Jessica made her way down the front staircase and headed for the basement. There she found Tim at the front of the choir room, where the Bible study class took place, going over the subject verses for that night's discussion—David versus Goliath.

"Are you ready?" Jessica asked.

Tim looked up, wondering which issue she might be referring. In his mind he knew the answer to both: no.

"As ready as I'll ever be, I guess."

"Did you have any luck last night?" she inquired.

"Uh, I found out a little bit of information, but I'll tell you about that later," he said as he gestured to the group of kids that were entering the room.

"Hey, guys," Tim said, welcoming the teenagers.

He did his best to mask the emotions that he felt. Something told him that this might be the last night he would ever see these kids or Jessica again.

The Bible study explored the position that David found himself in with the impending encounter with Goliath.

"Was David thinking to himself, *How did I get in this mess, and how do I get out of it?* Well, the Bible states that David put all of his faith in God and believed that God would deliver him through this," Jessica preached to the handful of teenagers.

Tim heavily studied the scriptures as Jessica read them aloud.

"Sometimes we find ourselves in situations that we cannot see or think a way out of. It's these times when we have to put all of our faith in God and know that he has a purpose for us," she said.

Tim looked up at Jessica and gave her a look that indicated that these were the words he needed to hear.

He cleared his throat and added to the conversation. "I know what you are thinking, guys. That sounds easier said than done, but it's those moments when all hope seems lost that you realize that only God can deliver you through it."

He stood up straight as if finding a new source of strength.

"Keep in mind, what God may have in store for you may not be exactly what you would think it would be. You just have to keep the faith in Him," he said. "Let's pray."

The Bible study ended with the normal, light conversation with the teenagers, and soon the choir room had emptied except for Tim and Jessica.

"Thanks for the message," Tim said with a smile. "I guess pastors can always benefit from hearing a message themselves."

Jessica returned the smile.

"I'm here to serve," she said with a small curtsey.

They walked to the church's main front doors.

"Is there anything I can do?" Jessica asked.

"Just pray," he answered, "and know that I love you."

Shocked that he said it and even more shocked to hear it in his own ears, Tim's heart stopped and then jumped as he had never felt it jump as Jessica quickly embraced him with all her might and whispered, "I'm glad!"

Not exactly the words Tim had hoped to hear, but they embraced and held on to each other without saying a word. Then reluctantly, he began to let go, but she held firm. He stopped and hugged her tight again with another squeeze.

He whispered, "You had better be going."

He could feel her hug deflate as she released her hold on him. She stepped back and placed her hand over his heart and softly patted his chest.

"You sure you don't want to talk about anything?" she asked.

"Nah, the lesson tonight really spoke to me. Everything will be fine," Tim replied.

He didn't want her to worry about him and the impending battle he had planned to find.

"Please be careful," she said.

Tim just nodded his head in agreement and excused himself as he went back into the church. Tim entered his room and locked the door. He pushed back the dresser and exposed the hidden door. He opened it and grabbed the black cloak that Jessica had made as well as the black sweatpants. He changed and threw on the cloak. Barefooted, he crawled into the dark corridor and placed the gold medallion around his neck. He paused as he waited for the full transformation to occur. He could feel his arms and legs grow as his chest began to swell along with the thick, callous pads forming on the bottom of his feet. With that came the eerie feeling of tickling goose bumps over his entire body as the hair began to grow. His back began to hunch as he wondered to himself if he would ever get used to this process.

Once the transformation completed, he looked around and found the old trap door that was used to bring in coal many years ago. Feeling amazed at his ability to see so well in the darkness, he reached up and popped the old door with relative ease. He peeked through the opening to make sure the coast was clear—no one in sight. So he threw the door open and crawled out. He continued to check for onlookers as he closed the trap door behind him. VoLt looked up at the full moon. It seemed fitting for a night like this. He quickly dashed in and out of the shadows of the buildings that surrounded the neighborhood.

As he made his way through the streets and alleys, he became aware that he could still smell Jessica's scent. Just like that night of the fire rescue. He recalled that he knew when she approached the alley where he hid by her smell alone.

He climbed a fire escape of a building and easily jumped the alley on the next building. As he ran across the rooftops, he glanced down and saw Jessica walking along the sidewalk. He wanted to go to her, but he knew he had a prior engagement that he had to attend, so he quickly passed her.

VoLt realized something. If he could locate Jessica from her scent, then maybe he could track Charles the same way. He knew that Charles's apartment was basically empty, but maybe there would be something there that would help him to track him down. He arrived at Charles's old apartment building just a few minutes later. He managed to climb down the side of the building using whatever gutters and water pipes were available. He reached the apartment window and looked in. It appeared that no one had taken up residence in the apartment yet, and even better, he found the window unlocked. VoLt opened the window and crawled inside. He quickly looked around the apartment. He entered the bedroom and opened the closet. To his surprise, one light-blue dress shirt hung in it.

Looking at the shirt, VoLt recalled the moment that Charles got the garment. It had been a birthday gift from Nancy just weeks before her death. VoLt seemed surprised that Charles would leave this behind. Then he realized the shirt had been left on purpose, intended for VoLt to find. He picked it up and smelled it and instantly captured the scent off of the shirt. He placed it back in the closet, crawled back out of the window, and climbed back to the rooftop.

Standing there, looking over the city skyline, VoLt could pick up on the trail of a scent that matched that of the shirt. He leaped off the building, landing on another smaller building adjacent to Charles's apartment, and then jumped to the street and began following the trail.

CHAPTER 25

As VoLt followed the scented trail, his stomach turned as he recognized the area. Scaling the side of a building using apartment windows as climbing tools, he reached the roof and scanned the neighborhood. From his view, he could easily see the Winchester Church. Taking a deep breath, he looked toward the church. A figure could be seen standing on the pitch of the roof.

The hairs on his back stood on end. His scowl tightened and he readied himself for battle. As he charged toward the church, he quickly prayed.

"Lord God Almighty, give me strength and courage to battle the evil I'm about to encounter!"

Reaching Winchester Church, he climbed the stone structure and reached the pitched room where he could see an impressive creature standing on the opposite end with his back to VoLt. Studying his physique, he could see that unlike his hunched over posture, this creature stood upright. Wearing a long black leather sleeveless coat, his exposed arms were covered in blond hair that somehow showcased his massive muscular build.

The beast's long blond flowing mane turned from side to side as he seemed to be awaiting someone's arrival.

"Evilution, I presume," VoLt growled.

The nearly six and a half foot creature spun around to face his adversary face-to-face. An evil smile slowly emerged.

"That would be correct," Evilution responded.

"Sporting a new look, Charles?"

"Yes, and as you can see, I've acquired a new outlook on life, just as you have. Right, VoLt?" Evilution responded with a glare. "Or should I say, Tim?"

"What have you done to yourself, Charles?" VoLt asked.

"You're one to talk!" Evilution shouted back.

"Need I remind you, you did this to me!" VoLt charged back.

"You're welcome," he sarcastically answered.

"But how?"

"How did I evolve into this? Oh, well, after I discovered your little secret. I knew you had the formula that Zen and I were searching for. Once I found it, I injected myself with it," Evilution explained. "Needless to say, I was aggravated when nothing happened. So I grabbed the capsule to throw it in anger when all of a sudden, things began to change. Discovering that the capsule was the trigger to my transformation, I just simply made these bracelets from the metal canister."

Evilution let out an evil chuckle.

"You should have seen the look on Zen's face when I showed up like this. And his reaction when he discovered I used all of the serum for this was priceless."

Appearing to be proud of his new physique, Evilution asked, "What do you think?"

"I think you need help," VoLt responded.

Evilution's smirk quickly turned to a scowl.

The two stood across from each other, standing on the long pitch of the church.

"What do you want?" VoLt growled.

"What do I want? What do I want?" Evilution yelled.

The question seemed to anger the blond creature.

"I had what I wanted, and it was taken away from me!" he yelled as he threw his large, fisted hands to the sky. "And if I can't have it all, then no one else will either!"

"What are you saying?" VoLt asked.

"Well, you tell me? Aren't all men created equal? And if they are to be equal, then shouldn't we all have the same loss?"

"You're twisting His words to comply with your own agenda?" he charged back.

"My agenda? I thought this was all His will and not ours!" Evilution argued.

"For someone who denounces the existence of God, you seem to be reciting His lines pretty well," VoLt responded.

"You sinned against me, brother!" Evilution yelled as he pointed his finger at VoLt.

"How?" VoLt asked.

"How? How about your other secret?" Evilution responded. "Just how long were you going to keep Jessica Parsons a secret from me?"

"I was trying to protect you!"

"Protect me? I don't need your protection!"

"I knew you wouldn't understand."

"Understand what?" Evilution asked.

VoLt hesitated for a second before he answered.

"I went on with my life! And Nancy would want you to go on with your life too!" he yelled back.

But the reference to Nancy struck a bad nerve in Evilution as he unleashed an angry roar and leaped through the air and attacked VoLt.

The force that Evilution brought with him caused VoLt to roll backward as Evilution kept his grip on VoLt, sending both of them in a backward somersault. Evilution released his grip and came out of the roll and landed on his feet. VoLt managed to get to his feet just as Evilution landed a hard punch to the left side of Volt's jaw. Then as VoLt tried to regain his stance, Evilution landed another punch to the right.

VoLt could feel the anger boil in him now. He finally gained his footing just as another left hook came at him. Catching Evilution's fist with his hand, VoLt saw the shock in his adversary's eyes as he squeezed his hand, letting Evilution know that their strengths were equally matched.

"Aren't you supposed to turn the other cheek? You know, roll over and grin and bear it?" Evilution asked.

"I don't have another cheek to turn!" VoLt roared as he delivered a thunderous right hand to Evilution's lower jaw. The impact sent Evilution staggering back, looking for his footing. VoLt pursued by delivering a backhanded slap just under Evilution's chin.

VoLt recognized the newly fashioned arm bracelets that Evilution was wearing and realized that those were the source of his strength, just as the gold medallion was the source of his own. He quickly went to remove the right one, but Evilution was not about to give them up yet. Evilution reached over and punched VoLt on the side of the head.

The punch to VoLt caused a loud ringing in his ear and a momentary loss of his balance.

Taking advantage of the moment, Evilution pulled a stone block from one of the pillars they were next to. He took the block with both hands and blasted VoLt on his back. VoLt dropped down to one knee in pain.

Quickly spinning around to face Evilution, VoLt tried to stand, but Evilution blasted him with another double-grip hit to the chest with the stone block.

VoLt staggered backward and fell on his back. He looked up to the starry sky and saw what appeared to be low-flying aircraft. Then he suddenly began to hear the wail of air sirens over the ringing in his head. VoLt realized the airplanes were Nazi bombers. As Evilution began to charge at him, he noticed the glow of numerous fires beginning to pop up along the city landscape.

He got to his feet just as Evilution charged. VoLt jumped in the air, swung his feet in front of him and landed a double-footed blast on the stone block that Evilution still carried. The force sent it back into Evilution's chest. Evilution growled in pain and landed on his back. VoLt quickly grabbed the stone block, and while standing over Evilution, he raised the block with both hands and with intentions of crushing Evilution when he realized what he was doing. He stopped and threw the block off the building.

"I won't do it!" he shouted at Evilution.

"Fine, then I will!" Evilution responded as he grabbed VoLt's ankle and twisted it, throwing VoLt off balance.

Evilution took this opportunity to push VoLt off the pitched peak. While VoLt staggered, Evilution attacked again with a series of left and right punches.

Evilution was now clearly on the offensive as VoLt reared in retreat from the devastating blows. VoLt swayed back and forth when Evilution landed a hard uppercut that snapped his head back, causing him to black out for a couple of seconds.

VoLt felt the sensation of sliding down the steep roof as he fought desperately to get his body to respond.

VoLt came to on the edge of the roof and managed to catch himself as his torso and legs dropped. VoLt hung on with all his might as he tried to regain his thoughts and strength. He looked up to the pitch of the rooftop. He could see Evilution staring down at him. As VoLt hung there, something caught his eye.

Off in the distance, VoLt recognized a single bomber coming back their direction. It was uncharacteristic for a Nazi plane to come back over the city after a bombing. As the plane drew closer, VoLt could see that the plane had one bomb left to drop. The wind blew in from the east, which covered the sound of the approaching plane from the west. Even Evilution with his highly tuned hearing didn't hear the incoming aircraft.

VoLt pulled himself up and pointed in the direction of the plane.

"Behind you!" he shouted at Evilution.

Evilution didn't heed the warning and refused to turn around. VoLt's heart jumped in his throat as he watched the bomb drop from the plane. Evilution turned around just in time to see the bomb hit the roof, erupting into a huge, thunderous explosion. VoLt turned and leaped off the building as it shook violently. When he landed, he quickly tucked in a ball and covered his head.

He could feel the vibrations of the church collapsing as he found himself buried under the rubble. VoLt didn't move until the ground stopped shaking. Covered under piles of rock,

VoLt managed to free himself and surveyed the destruction around him. Nothing but rubble remained. He ran around to the front, trying to find Evilution. He made his way through the destruction and found Evilution lying within a large pile of debris. Blood trickled from his mouth and on the side of his forehead. A steady stream of blood spilled out from the rocks under him. Evilution looked up at VoLt, still slightly conscious, his eyes still red with evil.

VoLt reached down and took off the metal bracelets from his wrist and witnessed the transformation from Evilution back into Charles. VoLt knelt down and placed his hand over his face.

"What are you doing?" Charles asked as he coughed blood.

"I'm trying to save you," VoLt replied as he placed his hand on Charles's face, allowing the evil to exit Charles and enter VoLt.

He had grown used to these cleansings and felt the expected burning sensation develop in his belly, but this time, the sensation appeared much darker and heavier. He stood up and released the bile, spinning his body around, spraying the hideous acid in a circle around him. As the bile touched the flames, it ignited, creating a ring of fire and burning off with a devilish hiss. But the flames didn't just hiss out; this time, they spoke.

"You will pay!"

VoLt stood motionless in fear at hearing the voice. The vapors quickly burned out, and the wall of fire disappeared with the shock of the demon's voice still ringing loud in VoLt's ears. He bent his head down and took off the medallion, allowing himself to transform back into Tim.

Tim walked over and saw Charles lying there, gasping for breath.

"Charles?" Tim said as he knelt down beside him, tears welling up in his eyes.

"Tim?" Charles asked as he turned his head to look at his old friend. "I'm sorry."

"Me too," Tim replied as he reached out and grabbed Charles's hand. "Let me get some help."

"No, no. Stay here," Charles said. "I have to warn you."

Charles coughed, and his face grimaced in pain.

"Zen...he's going to kidnap the prime minister...hold him for ransom for England's surrender," Charles said.

"What? Why?" Tim asked.

"Zen's a Nazi," Charles explained.

A cold flash of sweat quickly formed on Tim's back and head.

"The plan was to finish you"—he paused with guilt—"then meet Zen along with other Nazi agents, storm in, and kidnap Churchill. They have to be stopped," Charles said.

Tim's head spun with anxiety. Battling his best friend and trying to find Zen had spread him thin mentally already, but now the realization began to sink in that he now found himself in the middle of the war between England and Germany.

"Tim," Charles continued, gasping for breath. "Inside my coat pocket is a metal vile."

Tim reached inside Charles's coat pocket, pushing away various pieces of debris, and found the slender, metal container, dented but still intact.

"It's the last of the formula. Don't let Zen have it." Tears began to stream down Charles's face.

"Tim?" Charles called out again.

Tim could see the glazed look begin to come over Charles's face.

"I'm here," Tim said, squeezing his friend's hand.

"Forgive me."

"Okay." It's the only thing Tim could say between the tears that streamed down his face.

"Pray for me," Charles said as his grip starting to weaken.

"Charles, Charles!" Tim called out. "Oh, dear Lord. No! Save him!"

Charles slowly closed his eyes, and the weight of his head fell to the side as he let out his last breath.

"No…no…no," Tim cried as he held tight with both hands to Charles's lifeless hand.

As he knelt sobbing, he could hear the distant sirens of fire trucks approaching the scene. Tim stood up, wiping his nose with his forearm as he tried to refocus his mind. Looking down, he saw the two metal bracelets lying on the ground. He placed the vile inside his cloak pocket and then bent down and carefully picked up the bracelets, using the edges of his cloak so that his skin wouldn't come in contact with metal, and placed them inside another cloak pocket.

Looking down at his friend, guilt came over Tim as he realized he would have to leave him in this condition.

"I'm sorry, Charles."

Tim turned around and made his escape before the firefighters arrived at the scene.

A while later, a couple of blocks away in a telephone booth, Tim hung up the phone as a voice could still be heard asking questions on the other end. Tim quietly stepped out of the booth as he looked at the dark rooftops around him. Knowing Zen was close by, he patted his cloak pocket, reassuring himself he still had the medallion with him. He snuck across the street and slipped into a dark alley.

Hanging the medallion around his neck, he proceeded up the fire escape to the rooftop where Zen stood. VoLt peeked over the ledge. He found Professor Zen pacing back and forth on the opposite side of the roof. VoLt watched Zen check his watch while looking in the direction of one of the far-off, burning buildings. A fire burned in his belly as he had the man in sight that was to blame for so much turmoil in his life. Suddenly, he found himself charging towards Zen as his footsteps seem to alert the professor of his presence.

"Aww, finally, Evilution…" Zen said turning around.

VoLt could see the professor's eyes widen at the realization that it wasn't Evilution in his presence. The expression of confusion on Zen's face was quickly wiped away with VoLt's signature backslap across the professor's face.

The force caused Zen to spin around as he bent down to catch his balance on the rooftop's three-foot-high wall. Zen gazed down at the street six stories below him.

"Seriously, you need a new move," Zen said, rubbing his jaw. "Where's Evilution?"

VoLt didn't answer the question. Instead he walked over and grabbed Zen by the throat and pulled him close to his own face.

"It's over, Zen!" VoLt growled.

VoLt dragged Zen to the roof's wall that ran along all four edges of the rooftop and forced him to look down at the two cars that pulled up. Two men got out of the first car and ran back to the second and opened the back doors. Two other men in long, black coats and black hats stepped out. The two official-looking men glanced at the building and then looked at each other as if reaffirming that this was the right location.

Just as the four men started to approach the building, five police cars abruptly pulled up, only turning on the lights and sirens when they arrived. All four men held their arms up as the police apprehended them. One officer pulled the long coat off of one of the men, exposing the red Nazi band around his arm.

"Nicely played, young man," Zen said as he looked up at VoLt. "Okay, plan B. Now we both have a decision to make."

"What decision? You're about to be arrested. It's over," VoLt stated.

"Uh, not really. I anticipated that you might have defeated Evilution. So, just in case"—he paused as he watched the police officers run across the street to the building they stood on top of—"I have Nazi agents heading to your precious Jessica's apartment right now. If they don't hear from me in thirty minutes, they will take her."

"What? Take her?" VoLt asked.

"See, as mighty as you are, you're still vulnerable. So, allow me to escape, and I'll call off the dogs," Zen offered. "It was Charles's clever idea. Taking something so important to you in an effort to bring you to your knees."

"Also, I'll need the bracelets and your medallion," Zen demanded

"What?" VoLt asked.

"Yes, it was my formula, my idea, my work, my hardware," Zen said, holding out his hand.

"No."

"We don't have much time. Just give me the bracelets, and I'll be on my way, and your precious Jessica will be safe, for now." Zen looked down the rooftop edge as if counting the officers down on the street. "So do we have a deal? You let me go, and I'll let you go."

"What do you mean?" VoLt asked.

"If I go, your secret will be safe, Tim Warner," Zen said, "and so will your sweet Jessica."

VoLt began to pant slightly at the realization that Zen did, in fact, know his identity.

"But if I'm caught, you lose everything, including Jessica."

A quick sense of rage engulfed VoLt as he quickly found Zen in his grasp, dangling him over the edge to six stories below.

"What are you doing?" Zen asked as he held on to VoLt's arm out of obvious pain, not fear. "You're not going to kill me! You can't. It's against your faith."

VoLt's loud, beating heart nearly drowned everything out in his head, but the words of Zen rang louder. He didn't want to admit it, but Zen was right. VoLt couldn't kill the professor. And he wanted Jessica's safety more than anything else. He pulled Zen back in from the edge and released him.

Zen straightened his coat and smoothed back his blond, groomed hair. VoLt stood still and glared at his adversary. Unwilling to accept defeat just yet, and seeing the red glow of evil in Zen's eyes, he knew he had to do what he didn't want to do, save Zen's soul. VoLt began to slowly approach Zen again, but this time, extending his hand out.

"Professor, you have much evil in you. Let me help you."

Quickly, Zen pulled out his Ruger pistol and aimed at VoLt's head.

"Stop right there. Keep your hocus pocus trickery to yourself."

"There's no trickery, no magic, just God's love for you," VoLt replied with grinding teeth.

"Please, spare me," Zen said. "I'm not buying it. Besides, do you really want to save me?"

VoLt didn't say anything as he dropped his arm down.

"That's what I thought."

He felt ill inside at the realization that Zen was right.

"What's the plan?" VoLt asked as he dropped his head in embarrassment and defeat at having to bargain with a man like Zen.

"If I go, you'll never see me again, unless…" Zen paused.

"Unless what?" VoLt reluctantly asked.

"As long as VoLt never resurfaces after tonight, then I won't resurface."

"How can I trust you?" VoLt asked.

"You can't," Zen said. "But know this, my investors know who you are, and they might come calling."

"What do you mean by that?"

"Well, let's just say that they are intrigued with your capabilities and the source behind it." Zen paused.

VoLt turned and walked over to the ledge and looked over the city, but the only thing he saw was the life he currently had quickly slipping away from his grip.

The echoes of the demonic voice he heard at the burning rubble rang in his ears. He felt like he was indeed paying for it with every fiber of his soul.

"Go," VoLt regretfully, said pointing to the fire escape.

"Good boy," Zen replied. "I'll just take the bracelets, and I'll be on my way," Zen said as he held out his hands.

"No. Now go!"

"I want those bracelets!"

"You don't get it! We both lose here! We both lose everything that is our own heart's desire! Go!" VoLt barked as they could hear the footsteps rapidly approaching the staircase to the rooftop.

Zen pulled out his pocket watch and glanced at the time. "Looks like you and Jessica are on your own now."

VoLt roared at Zen, turned, and leaped off the building into darkness.

VoLt ran as fast as he could toward Jessica's apartment. He didn't know how many Nazis he would encounter, let alone what he would or could do. Tim realized that the life he had and the life he wanted appeared to be slipping away with every step he took. He knew he would have to make the most difficult decision of his young life, a decision he knew he would regret for the rest of his life.

CHAPTER 26

With his heart racing, VoLt quickly made his way toward Jessica's apartment. His head throbbed with pain, along with the astonishing amount of information. The death of Charles and the realization of Professor Zen's association with Nazi Germany appeared to be more than this young man could handle. Now his love was in danger. Just mere months ago, he had arrived at Berthel Church as young man fresh out of the seminary with his whole life ahead of him. Now it all seemed to be dashing away.

VoLt reached Jessica's neighborhood. Looking down from the rooftops, he located two cars that contained four men each. He knew they didn't have much time. Locating Jessica's window, he could see light coming from within. Leaping from one roof to the next, he landed and skidded to a stop on the pads of his feet. Carefully climbing down the building to the third floor of the four-story building, he pounced into her window. The room appeared to be empty.

"Jessica?" he growled out. Realizing that his low roar might scare her, he quickly took off the medallion and transformed back into Tim.

"Jessica, are you here?"

Cautiously, Jessica peeked from her bedroom with a terrified look on her face.

"Tim, is that you? What is it? What's wrong? Are you okay?" she asked as she ran over and embraced him. Then shock overcame her as she saw the purple bruises on his face. "You're hurt!"

"Shhh," he responded. He tried to get her to calm down before her neighbors became alarmed.

"I'm fine, but"—he paused, trying to muster the strength to tell her—"we're in danger."

"What do you mean?" she asked.

"Professor Zen knows about us. He knows I'm VoLt and knows about you," he said. He dropped his head in embarrassment and regret. "There are Nazi agents waiting outside to take you."

"What? Nazis? Why? What do we do?" she fearfully asked as she looked at him with hope that he had an answer.

"We have to get you somewhere safe," he began. "It's not safe for you here. They will find you and hurt you to get to me, and I can't let that happen."

They quickly gathered some of her basic essentials and shoved them in a suitcase. As they quickly packed, Tim told her about the battle with Evilution and the death of Charles. Tears streamed down her face as she realized that Tim could have been on the opposite end of the way things turned out and knew that the perfect life that she had been dreaming about with Tim was in serious jeopardy.

"Okay, we better go!" Tim said as he picked up the suitcase. They made their way out of the apartment. As he opened the apartment door, he met three men in long, black coats.

"Mr. Warner, I presume?" a man asked with a heavy German accent.

Jessica screamed, and Tim went to slam the door just as one of the Nazis grabbed the door and began to force it open. Tim quickly dug in his pocket and grabbed the medallion. The rapid transformation gave him the strength to slam the door on the German's hand.

The Nazi yelled in pain as VoLt could hear the soldiers scrambling for their pistols. VoLt opened the door and attacked. He punched the man square in the jaw that had been clutching his hand in pain, then grabbed the pistol of one agent and forcing it down while kicking the third agent in the chest as he aimed his revolver at VoLt. Then VoLt landed a hard fist across the nose of the assailant that he had a hold of by the gun. Grabbing the pistol, he dismantled it with relative ease. The three men lay there either unconscious or grimacing in intense pain.

"Time to go!" VoLt growled as he grabbed Jessica by the hand and led her upstairs to the rooftop before the other Nazi agents arrived on the scene.

VoLt tossed her suitcase with relative ease over the alley and onto the adjacent building. "Hold on!" VoLt said as he picked up Jessica and began running across the rooftop. He leaped into the air and soared across the alley below. Skidding to a stop, they ran to the building's fire escape and made their way down safely.

"Where to now?" she asked.

"To the only man I trust right now," Tim said as he took off the medallion, allowing the transformation to take place.

They reached the modest home of Pastor Canow. Tim did not feel good about having to wake the pastor, let alone having to divulge everything to him. He knocked on the door and waited a minute, and then he knocked again. This time, a light came on from the back of the house, more than likely from the kitchen. Then the living room light came on, and the pastor opened the door.

"Tim, is that you?" he asked.

"Yes, sir, it is," Tim answered humbly.

The pastor quickly opened the door to let him in.

"Miss Parsons?" he asked.

"Yes, sir," she said in the same humble tone.

As they entered the living room, the pastor asked, "Is everything okay?"

"Honestly, no," Tim replied.

The pastor's wife entered the living room with concern on her face. She quickly walked over to a noticeably distressed Jessica in a gesture of support.

After taking a deep breath, Tim told the pastor everything, including the night that he was injected with the collective plasma and his battles with Evilution, Professor Zen, and the Nazis. Then he told him of his budding romance with Jessica. The pastor, being the constant man of integrity, listened without throwing judgment on anybody.

"So, sir, is it okay if Jessica stays here until we know that Zen and the Nazis are no longer a threat to her?" Tim asked.

"Why, yes, of course. My wife always has a room prepared for emergencies," the pastor replied. "What about you, Tim? What are you going to do?"

"I have to leave," he said as he turned to look at Jessica, "and I can't come back."

Tears began to fall from Jessica's eyes.

"No! Why?" she asked.

"Jessica, I lost Charles. I couldn't save him, and I can't bear to watch anything happen to you."

"We can work something out! I'll go with you. Wherever you go, I'll go with you!" she pleaded.

He knelt down beside her. "You can't. As much as I want to run away with you, you can't go with me. As long as I'm never seen again and VoLt never reappears, I know that you'll be safe."

He reached in and gave her a hug and whispered in her ear, "Always know that I love you."

He stood up and shook the pastor's hand, "Thank you, thank you for everything, sir."

"It was a privilege to work with you, son," the pastor replied.

The pastor's eyes shifted in the area around him as if trying to think of a way to help Tim.

"Where are you going?" Jessica asked through her tears and gasping breaths.

"I'll let you know when I think things are safe, but until then, I need to keep that to myself," he said, knowing that he might never be able to communicate with Jessica again.

"I have something for you," Jessica said as she tried to compose herself. "I want to give this to you." The tears continued between sniffles with her nose. "Something to remember me by."

She reached for his hand and placed a golden pocket watch in his palm. Tim didn't say a thing; he just opened it up to see the picture of Jessica inside. He fought back the tears and gave her one last hug before he walked out the door without looking back.

CHAPTER 27

Back in his living quarters, Tim gathered his things and placed them in the suitcase. Luckily, he didn't have much to pack and hadn't accumulated much during his nearly seven-month service. He took a small wooden crate and placed the various newspaper articles that reported on the creature's sightings. Then with a heavy heart he placed the gold pocket watch that contained Jessica's picture in the crate. Even though she had just given it to him, he couldn't take it with him. Tears fell down his face as he shoved the wooden crate in the rafter of the tunnel that hid behind his dresser. He closed the door and then moved the dresser back in place, completely covering the small door. He picked up his suitcase, turned off the light, and closed the door behind him.

The seven a.m. train arrived right on schedule. Tim somberly watched the train pull in. The call for "all aboard" rang out, and Tim reluctantly picked up his suitcase and boarded the train. He took his seat and prepared himself for a long, three-hour ride to the northern region of England to his hometown of Jennings. Guilt consumed him for letting Professor Zen escape. He vowed that he would do whatever he could to repay the debt he created by not stopping Zen. Tim knew what he had to do.

He also took full responsibility for Charles and for the heartbreak that Jessica was enduring. He hoped that eventually she would forgive him and move on to have a rewarding life, but the pain in his heart made it unbearable to envision her with anyone else but him.

He prayed to himself, "Forgive me, Father, for what I have done."

The train car jolted as the locomotive slowly began to move away from the station. Tim's heart sank even more at the realization that he was leaving the life he thought the Lord had planned for him. He had never felt more lost and alone.

Once he made it home, he simply told his family that things were not working out as he had hoped. Seeing and living through the Nazi air raids, he realized that he needed to serve in another capacity—joining the military and fighting Nazi Germany. After much discussion with his parents, he enlisted with the royal army and left two weeks later for training, with Jessica constantly on his mind.

CHAPTER 28

Dustin sat motionless, trying to make sense of the story he had just heard. Tim seemed to be of sound mind, but now, Dustin began questioning that. It seemed so unreal. The doubts began to flood his mind along with a valid question.

"Miss Parsons can verify this story?" Dustin asked.

"Yes, she could, but she swore she would never tell anybody," Tim answered.

Noticing the mental struggle going on inside Dustin, Tim attempted to go back to his farming chores within the barn.

Dustin wondered if he should just grab his backpack and leave. He couldn't believe he wasted a whole day on this wild goose chase. He tried to make sense of it all, but he just couldn't. Dustin could almost hear the laughter of the doubters in his head.

"We told you so! You're wasting your time!" they shouted.

"If you don't mind, I'll think I'll go make some tea. I'm a little parched from talking so much," Tim said.

"Yeah, yeah, sure. I'll wait here," Dustin said.

Dustin sat there for a few minutes in silence until he saw Tim coming back, carrying a tray with a hot pot of tea. He came back wearing an old, oversized, green army poncho. Tim sat the tray on the workbench.

"Looks like rain?" Tim said.

"Yep," Dustin said as he knelt down slightly to look at the sky.

"Do you like sugar with your tea?" Tim asked.

"Yes, thank you," Dustin replied.

Tim poured Dustin a cup and handed it to him and then slid the jar of sugar in front of Dustin. Dustin dipped two spoonfuls into his cup and stirred. He blew on the tea and then tipped it up to sip it. It tasted horrible. Trying not to be rude, Dustin covered his dislike by adding more sugar.

"Okay, you got me. I have a bit of a sweet tooth," Dustin said as he poured six more spoonfuls into the cup.

The sugar didn't help much, but it allowed him to power through the disgusting taste until he finished it.

"Thank you," Dustin said as he placed the empty cup on the tray and turned to look out the barn door at the countryside. He didn't want Tim to see him trying with all his might to keep the tea down.

Tim continued to sit, sipping his tea.

"Pretty countryside, isn't it?" Tim asked.

"Uh, yes it is," Dustin replied as he started to gaze upon the view.

Tim placed his tools back in their proper spots. He grabbed an old leather satchel that hung from a hook just above the worktable and flung it over his shoulder.

"Come on, I'll show you around," Tim said as he motioned to Dustin to follow him through a wooden section of the farm.

Reluctantly, Dustin followed while mumbling under his breath. "Why not, I've already wasted the whole day. A pointless walk through the farm should be about fitting."

The sun began to set as they walked through the woods. Tim started talking about current events that had been in the news, ranging from the 9/11 attacks on the United States to the London bombing attacks in 2005.

"It reminds me of those days during World War II. There's so much evil out there," Tim said.

Dustin just nodded an acknowledgement as he continued to struggle with the story that Tim had told him previously. Dustin knew the current world events as well as the current struggles of other individuals that don't necessarily make the evening news.

"Do you ever feel overwhelmed with your position?" Tim asked.

"What do you mean?" Dustin replied.

"You know. You hear all these problems that people are having, and all you can offer to them is, 'I'll pray for you'"

"Well, yeah. Sometimes I wish there was something more I could do, but I'm limited to what I can do," Dustin replied.

Dustin wondered about the direction of this conversation. He felt a smidge of relief knowing that Tim seemed to understand the challenges of being a servant of God. He often struggled internally with his limitations. He wanted to do more for those in need.

While Dustin pondered his dilemma, he didn't see Tim reach into his satchel and pull out a cloth-covered article. Dustin walked around a bit with his head down, as the doubts seemed to be getting the best of him. Then he heard Tim make a grunt-like noise. He looked over and found himself frozen in fear as he witnessed Tim transform into the hideous beast.

Dustin jumped and began running for his life through the woods. Darkness had begun to settle in, which made his escape that much more difficult. He could hear himself pant in panic as he feverishly tried to recall the path they took. Behind him, he could hear the creature snort louder and louder as he closed in on Dustin.

Suddenly Dustin felt the grasp of the monster's hand on his right shoulder and then felt the instant thud of his body landing hard on his back against the ground. The impact caused Dustin to have the wind knocked out of him. Gasping for air, he looked up and saw the aged creature stand over him. Dustin passed out as the creature bent down to pick him up.

An intense pain in Dustin's arm caused him to wake up, only to find the creature holding him down as he injected a fluid into Dustin's right arm.

"What are you doing to me?" Dustin cried out.

The creature was silent. He emptied the contents of the syringe and pulled out the needle.

"Aghhh!" Dustin screamed.

The beast released Dustin from his clutch as Dustin quickly jumped to his feet and grabbed his right arm with his left, all the while still feeling the soreness in his back. He also noticed his shirt had been removed.

"What did you do?" Dustin demanded.

Silence fell on the woods for a moment while Dustin waited for a response, acutely aware that his fear of the creature had now turned to anger.

"I did what I had to do," Tim said as he reached up and took off the gold *V* medallion.

Dustin watched as Tim transform back into himself.

"I know you don't understand, but I've been praying for someone to show up to take up the mantle of VoLt," Tim explained.

"What?" It was the only thing Dustin could ask.

Tim walked over to Dustin and hung the medallion around his neck. Tim stood back and watched the transformation take place to Dustin's body. Dustin groaned as he felt his arms extend down to the ground as the muscles in his chest and back swelled and tightened. He hunched over, and then the explosion of hair covered his body until a large, nearly black mane formed around his head.

The newly transformed Dustin stood in front of Tim. The creature growled and glared at him.

A sense of relief came over Tim as he stood face-to-face with his new protégé.

"It nice to finally meet you, VoLt, Vigilante of Lord's treasures."

CHAPTER 29

Two days later, Dustin sat on the train heading back to London, and recalled the events in his head. He had spent the last couple of days learning about his newly acquired abilities. His anger toward Tim had subsided. Tim apologized for doing what he did and the manner in which he had done it. Tim explained to Dustin that he knew Dustin wouldn't be open to accepting his request to take up the banner for VoLt freely.Tim knew it would have to be forced on Dustin, much like Tim had it forced on him that fateful, stormy fall night back in 1940.

Unconsciously rubbing his arm in the spot of the injection, Dustin recalled asking Tim why he didn't do more with this ability. Tim explained to him why he made the choices he did. Tim realized that he failed serving God the way he should have served as VoLt. He couldn't forgive himself for the death of Charles or the failure to capture Professor Zen when he had the chance. His love for Jessica and concern for her safety clouded his judgment. Tim's only escape was joining the army and fighting the Nazis.

During the war, he had seen the concentration camps in Poland. Tim had witnessed firsthand the gruesome evilness that lay in the hearts of the Nazi regime. Unfortunately, by the time his unit had arrived, they were too late. It had become another failure in Tim's mind.

Dustin's mind flashed back to when he boarded the train. He recalled asking Tim if he ever served as VoLt again after that last confrontation with Zen. Tim hadn't replied to the question; he had just given a small smile and a hug.

"Good luck to you, son, and God bless," Tim said as he let go and quickly disappeared amid the crowded station.

Dustin finally returned home to the Berthel Church. He gazed at the soft glow of the stained-glass windows against the evening's darkness. He felt comfort come over him as he walked up the steps to the church. It truly did feel like home now. As he entered the sanctuary, he felt surprised to see Miss Parsons sitting in her normal spot, all alone.

Approaching her from behind, she turned around in her seat to greet Dustin.

"Welcome home!" she said.

"Thank you, Miss Parsons," he said. Then he asked the obvious question. "What brings you here so late at night?"

"Well, the pastor told me that you would be coming home this evening. I just wanted to hear how the visit went."

A little exhausted from the trip and everything else, he really didn't have it in him to discuss the details with her, but he couldn't blame her for her curiosity. *She's waited her whole life to hear from Tim, so why should she wait any longer?*

Dustin recalled the conversation with Tim regarding Jessica. Tim had insisted that Dustin keep his new ability a secret from Jessica. The less she knew, the better. Dustin did inform her that Tim had been working on the family farm since he came back from the war. Jessica asked why Tim didn't return to her. Dustin said that Tim's sense of failure kept him away from the ministry and everything else. He vowed to concentrate on the family business as a form of his own penance.

Miss Parsons began to weep.

"Oh, Tim, why?" she said as she looked up.

"Miss Parsons, believe me, as hard as the war and the death of his friend Charles were on him, the hardest thing for him was leaving you."

Unknowingly, Dustin exposed another issue. Miss Parsons jump at the opportunity for the other subject.

"He told you about Charles?"

"Yes."

Dustin quickly recognized the angle of her next impending question.

"Did he tell you how he died?"

"He told me that he died during a Nazi air raid," he answered as a small breakout of sweat formed on his back, a natural reaction of Dustin's when he was trying to withhold something or lying.

"That's it?" she asked.

He nodded his head yes. Dustin searched his brain for something to steer away from VoLt.

"He kept the pocket watch," Dustin said, trying to bring her some comfort.

"I'm glad," she said as she stood up from the pew.

She fastened the buttons on her dark-gray, woolen coat and picked up her purse. "Well, it's getting late, and I'm sure you're tired," she said.

"Aw, I'm all right."

"Well, thank you for visiting with me," she said.

"Anytime. My door is always open, Miss Parsons."

"You can call me Jessica."

"Yes, ma'am," he said with a smile.

The friendly banter put a smile on her face too. She patted him on the shoulder and made her way to the back of the church. Guilt consumed him for keeping things from her. But he felt he had to. He had to protect both of them. Seeing her exit, he realized he couldn't let her walk home this late at night by herself. Dustin quickly caught up with her and walked her home. Along the way, Miss Parsons reminisced about the walks she and Tim would take together.

CHAPTER 30

Dustin stood still at his dresser as he continued to recall the events that had led to his newfound capabilities and made him the apparent heir of the monstrous curse. At least that's how Dustin saw it.

He didn't ask for this. He simply went up there to make a wrong, right. Dustin's original intentions were to return some items to the rightful owner as well as have some questions answered from the previous tenant of his quarters.

Dustin let out a heavy sigh as he looked at himself in the mirror. It had been an exhausting couple of months. He knew the job of being a youth minister would be challenging, and he had mentally prepared himself to be pushed to the limit. Trying to rebuild the youth movement in a church was challenging in itself, but there was no way that he could have psychologically prepared himself to be chosen to bear the cross that had been laid on him.

On his first outing as the creature, he had managed to put a stop to the bullying that Cameron had been a victim of at the hands of Kevin and his two buddies, Cass and Chet. He hoped that after this encounter with Kevin, they would no longer be a menace to him.

During his small training session with Tim, Tim revealed to Dustin the ability to draw the evil out of those who were consumed with the sins that kept them from making rational decisions. But despite the fact that they had been freed of the evil clutch, that didn't necessarily mean they were free from it forever. He explained that people were all susceptible to their own free will. People were free to choose their own actions, whether they were right or wrong.

That's the lesson that Tim had learned from Charles. Despite the fact that VoLt did relieve Charles of the evil that consumed him after Nancy's death, it was ultimately Charles's decision to fall victim again to his own jealousy. His thirst for revenge had been fueled after he discovered that Tim was in fact VoLt and had a love of his own in Jessica. Charles's failure had come about when he chose to follow his need to make things equal in his own demented mind by inflicting pain on those who had what he wanted. This decision ultimately led him to his own death.

Dustin also realized that, on a certain level, he had been able to help ease the burden that Tim had been carrying with him all these years. If nothing else, just being there and allowing Tim to tell someone why he had left the way that he did back in the spring of 1941 must have helped. Dustin felt the deep admiration and love that Tim still had for Jessica.

Dustin took a drink of water. He felt a little drained after reliving all the events in his head. He focused the rest of the day, preparing for the Bible study later that day. He took his work seriously and became fully enthralled in it, so much so that he would lose track of time. Dustin looked at the clock and realized that it was nearly time for it to start. He grabbed his Bible and notebook and headed for the choir room.

As he entered the room, he wasn't surprised to see Cameron already there, sitting on the floor and waiting for Dustin to arrive.

"Good evening, Cameron," he greeted him with a smile. "How's everything going?"

"Great!" Cameron replied. "Everything's going really well here lately."

Dustin needed to hear the validation that VoLt had made a positive impact on some level. Maybe, just maybe, he was on to something.

"That's good to hear," Dustin replied as he opened the door and flicked on the lights.

They both took their normal seats as Dustin gathered his notes together. He frequently looked at the door, expecting Abbey to come in at any moment. Despite the fact that she still attended at the request of her father, she was still dependable to show up. She had actually begun to participant more freely in the discussion during the classes.

A few minutes passed, and it appeared that Abbey was not going to attend this night's Bible study. Reluctantly, Dustin began the class. He had to admit to himself that his head was not solely on the lesson, feeling preoccupied with why Abbey hadn't shown up. The hour passed by slowly and eventually closed with just Dustin and Cameron ending it in prayer.

As he gathered his things and made casual conversation with Cameron, he could hear footsteps come quickly down the stairs. It was Abbey, and she didn't look like her normal self. Dustin quickly examined her and realized that she had been in some kind of struggle. Her hair was a mess when it usually looked perfect. Her sleeves were ripped, and her knees were dirty and scraped.

"Abbey, are you okay?" asked Cameron.

"What happened?" Dustin asked as he ran to her side.

The tear stains streaked down her dirty face. She tried to catch her breath before she tried to tell them.

"We went to this party," she began to explain. She had difficulty looking the youth minister in the face. "And we had this punch. Then next thing I knew, I started feeling a little woozy. That's when these boys grabbed us and dragged us into a dark room."

She began to tear up as she remembered the events.

"It was dark. I couldn't see anything." She wiped the tears from her eyes. "This one boy kept trying to…"

Abbey paused, as she couldn't finish the sentence.

"That's when I began to fight him off. I kicked and punched till I was free of him. I crawled around till I found the door and escaped."

Catching her breath and swallowing tears, she continued, "My friends are still in there. I couldn't help them. I couldn't help them!"

Dustin reached out and placed his hand on her upper back in an attempt to help Abbey calm down.

"I didn't know where to go. I was scared. This was the first place I ran to," Abbey explained.

"Where is this party?" Dustin asked in a low, growling tone that even caught Cameron's attention.

"It's over on Mancastle, three blocks over," Abbey told him.

"Cameron, take Abbey to the police," Dustin ordered.

"Okay," Cameron replied, surprised at the sudden task of responsibility.

"What are you going to do?" he asked, turning around toward Dustin only to see him run out of the room and out of sight.

CHAPTER 31

The music blared from the bottom flat of a dilapidated apartment building. The flat was packed with partygoers of all kinds. In a dark bedroom off the living room, the door was closed and locked. The music from the living room came in muffled as it seeped in through the bedroom door and walls.

Then a voice inside the dark room asked, "Hey, Chet, you awake?"

"Uh, yeah…just high as a kite," answered Chet. "How about you?"

"Oh yeah," he responded.

"Hey, Robb?" Chet asked. "Do you think it's kicked in with the girls yet?"

"Do you hear them crying now?" Robb replied with a sarcastic tone.

"No, but, man, they were really fighting it!"

"Yeah, they needed something to calm them down," Robb said.

Then another voice interrupted the conversation, "You guys should have let them go, you know."

"Ah, you're just bummed because yours got away, Cass." Chet chuckled.

"No sense in wasting any more time. Come here, my love," Chet said as he pulled one of the girls toward him.

The girl began to cry and moan as she still tried to fight off her assailant, but she was too incapacitated to defend herself.

From the living room, the muffled party sound changed abruptly. The music stayed the same, but conversations quickly went silent as the sound of footsteps and commotion could be heard going out the door.

"Hey, what's goin' on out there?" Cass asked his friends as he attempted to get up to investigate.

Just then, an object came crashing through the wall from the living room and slammed against the opposite bedroom wall, causing Cass to take cover by rolling over on his side and covering his head.

"What the in the world?" Chet shouted.

Robb jumped to his feet to see a large hole in the wall. They were shocked to see that a buddy of theirs had been the object that came crashing through the wall and landed unconscious on the floor. Robb turned around to see what caused it, only to be face-to-face with a creature that he'd never seen before.

"Oh my—" was all that Robb could utter before the creature reached through the hole with his enormous, long arms, grabbed Robb by the chest of his shirt, and flung him over his shoulder like a piece of trash. The force sent him across the living room as he landed on top of the entertainment center, which caused the stereo system to blow, sending light-blue electric shocks out of it. Robb then rolled off and landed on the floor, wincing in pain.

Then the creature walked over to Chet, who sat motionless in fear. VoLt could see the fear welling up in his eyes.

He reached down, grabbed him, picked him up, and stared into his eyes.

"I don't believe she wanted to be entertained by you," VoLt said.

VoLt threw the thug against the wall, leaving a deep impression. Chet landed on the ground, knocked out cold.

VoLt then turned around and proceeded to confront the third assailant.

He could hear the distant sounds of police sirens approaching.

Then he heard the third thug say, "Please, please don't hurt me again."

Surprised by the request, VoLt focused on the man curled up in a ball. He looked down and felt shocked to see Cass, one of the three thugs that had bullied Cameron.

VoLt knew he was running out of time, so he picked up Cass and looked him square in the eyes.

"No, I won't hurt you, but you're going to make this right," VoLt ordered as he looked around the room, addressing the two young girls that had now found each other and were huddled together in fear.

"If you don't make this right, then you'll be seeing me again."

A light rain started to fall down on the crowd as they formed in front of the building where the party had been going on. The crowd waited in anticipation for the police to arrive. They heard the sirens coming for blocks. The crowd consisted of fellow building residents, bystanders, and even some of the party participants. Those who had stuck around appeared to be the ones that were innocent of any illegal activity. They were eager to give an account of the party's events if needed.

"What was that thing?" was a question that could be overheard several times.

The police finally arrived in a squad of five police cars. Three officers stormed the basement flat. Along with the three assailants, they also found two girls huddled together, crying and shaking. The officers could tell that they had been assaulted by the rips in their clothing and cuts and bruises on their faces and arms. They found one of the assailants that appeared to be very distraught about the evening's activities.

"Don't worry, ladies. We're the police. You'll be safe now," one of the officers stated.

One of the officers walked over to Cass, who was still huddled in a ball in the corner.

"Are you all right, lad?" the cop asked.

"No," the young man replied, rocking back and forth in a cradle position. "I'm definitely not all right."

"Can you tell me what happened here?"

"Yes, I have to tell you," Cass said as tears started streaming down his face. "We forced these girls after they got drunk on the punch we spiked. Then we were going to have our way with them, but we were stopped."

"What stopped you?" asked the cop.

"I don't know what he is. All I know is that I don't want to see him again," the young man answered.

"What's your name, and who else is in on this?" the cop asked.

"My name is Cass, and those two over there were in on it," Cass answered, pointing to his two friends and implicating them along with himself.

"Can you tell me more about this thing that stopped you?" another officer asked as he looked around the apartment, examining the large hole in the wall.

VoLt stood on the rooftop of an adjacent building from where all the activity took place. He felt his stomach turning and knew he had to vomit. He leaned over and released the bile out of his mouth. He inhaled a large breath and then spit out the remaining bits. He pulled out a match and struck it against a leather strip that had been sewn on the inside of the cloak. The match sparked and flickered into a small flame. Bending down and dropping the match on the bile, VoLt stood back and watched it ignite in a quick ball of purple flames only to be quickly doused out by the rain that had started to fall.

He turned around and looked over the balcony in time to watch the police place the three thugs in the squad cars. He scanned the crowd and saw Abbey and Cameron waiting to find out the status of her friends.

Just as Cass was about to be placed in the squad car he recognized Cameron standing in the crowd. "Just ask him! He's seen him!" Cass yelled, nodding his head in Cameron's direction since his hands were cuffed behind his back.

"Just get in the car, lad," the cop said as he placed Cass in the squad car.

Another officer walked over to Cameron.

Looking at him suspiciously, he asked, "So, you've seen this creature too?"

"Creature?" Cameron asked.

"Yeah, some kind of creature—looks half-gorilla, half-man and wears a medallion in a shape of a *V*?" the officer said.

"Uh, yes I have," Cameron answered, feeling guilty to expose his personal crusader. "But I do believe his intentions are good, not evil," Cameron said, trying to defend his new friend.

"Well, we'll decide that," the officer said. "I'd like for you to come down to the station for more questioning."

"Am I in trouble?" Cameron asked.

"No, not at all, but the more information you can provide, the better," the officer answered.

Cameron followed the officer to the squad car as VoLt watched from the rooftop above. An uneasy feeling came over VoLt. His intentions were only to help, but it seemed that the authorities had become more interested in the creature itself as opposed to stopping the onslaught of drugs and forced sex on teenagers.

He watched the squad car drive off with Cameron in it. Then he saw Abbey's two friends come walking out. They were wrapped in blankets as Abbey ran to them and embraced them both. They stood there for a few moments, holding each other until a paramedic insisted that they get in the ambulance so they could be taken care of at the hospital. VoLt felt pleased to see the girls walking out on their own power. At least it was something he could be pleased about.

CHAPTER 32

The sun peeked through the clouds, drying off the streets and sidewalks from the early morning rain. A man in a fine, tan, Italian suit sat at a table in a small café, sipping coffee and reading the *London Times*, occasionally stroking his smoothly trimmed moustache. A waitress walked over to his table.

"More coffee?" she asked as she glanced over the fifty-year-old man with slight hint of gray entwined with his light-brown hair.

"Yes," the man answered but offered no gratitude for her service.

"Looks like it's going to be a nice day today." The waitress attempted to start a pleasant dialogue with her customer as she poured him his coffee.

"Just another day," the man replied without lifting his head from the paper.

The waitress became aware that the man was not the small-talk type and decided to leave him alone.

He scanned over the articles, seemingly looking for something that he might find worth reading. Article title after article title bored him, but then something caught his attention. He did a double take as he reread the story's title: "Party Has the Ultimate Crasher."

The man read the article, and as he did so, his grip on the paper tightened. He abruptly folded the paper and slammed it down on the table. He quickly gulped his coffee, stood up, and grabbed the paper once again and rolled it up tightly, carrying it like a nightstick. The man abruptly proceeded towards the door.

The waitress noticed his quick departure and attempted to address him before he left. "Excuse me, sir, but…"

The man kept walking without acknowledging her presence.

"Excuse me, sir!" she attempted again to get his attention, but he continued to ignore her as he stormed out the door.

"What a jerk!" she said out loud, and she watched him walk down the sidewalk without glancing back, leaving his tab unpaid.

Dustin walked through the pews, straightening out the hymnals that were placed sideways or upside down from the previous service. He didn't mind doing the menial tasks. He believed that the menial tasks helped him to stay grounded and humble, which he believed was important in the career path that he had elected to take or was called to take.

A feeling came over him that he was being watched. He looked up and saw Miss Parsons standing about seven rows back. He was surprised to see her, but more surprised to see the look on her face, a scornful glare he had never seen her deliver to anyone.

"Jessica, is everything okay?" he asked. He felt like a little boy who had been caught with his hand in the cookie jar.

"Can you explain this?" she asked as she handed him the paper with the story of the party crasher on top.

He took a moment to glance at the paper, which reported on VoLt's activity from the previous night. Dustin became shocked at the details of VoLt's appearance, even down to the gold *V* medallion. The article mentioned that three arrests were made that night and reported on the two girls who were assaulted. The article did not make the connection that the creature had arrived to save the girls, only that it had caused heavy damage to the apartment and terrified the citizens that it encountered.

He looked up at Jessica, but he didn't have a reply.

"I'll ask you again, did you and Tim discuss anything else on your visit with him?" she asked.

She continued looking sternly at him while he searched for the right answer. Then Jessica asked the question that she already knew the answer to. "And, have you taken up a part-time job?"

Dustin couldn't bring himself to look Jessica in the eyes. He wanted to keep this from her, mainly for her own safety, but he knew she wasn't the kind to let something like this to go without discussion. He knew he had to divulge everything to her.

At the police station, in the holding cell, sat a group of men who were waiting for the consequences of the previous night's activities. Three of the men sat together. The effects of sobering up resulted in pounding headaches, along with the bumps and bruises caused by their uninvited guest.

They began to realize the possible repercussions of their actions. The assault on the three girls would result in a more harsh punishment than their other run-ins with the authorities. They sat there as they waited for the consequences to begin.

"Man, I can't believe you ratted us out!" Robb growled at Cass.

"Hey, what we did was wrong! And besides, I didn't want that creature coming back for me," Cass responded.

An officer came to the cell and looked disgustedly at Robb and Chet, as he could tell they were starting to sober up.

"Hey," the officer barked in a low voice, "you have a visitor here to speak to you two."

Chet and Robb looked at each other in disbelief that they would know someone who cared if they were here or not.

"Come on, you two! Up on your feet!" the officer barked again, showing he had no patience for the two young men.

"Hey, what about me?" Cass asked.

"What about you?" the officer barked back. "You weren't invited."

The two of them got up and tried to shake off the clouds still lingering in their heads. The officer opened the cell door and escorted the two men down a hallway to a room that the police used for questioning.

The officer opened the door and directed Chet and Robb to enter. In the room sat a gentleman dressed quite nicely in his tan suit and Fedora hat.

"Come on in, boys," the gentleman said. "Sit right down."

Chet looked over at Robb, who looked back at him as they tried desperately to recall if they knew this man.

"Looks like you boys have been living a little rough lately," the man said as he surveyed their appearances.

He recognized the bruises on the faces of both of them.

"Yeah, we kind of had a rough night," Robb answered as he rubbed the back of his neck.

"That's what I would like to talk to you about," the gentleman said.

"Are you a cop or something?" asked Chet in an agitated tone.

"No"—the man laughed—"not hardly."

He quickly became serious again. "I'm interested in the thing that did this to you."

Chet looked over at Robb to see if they wanted to recall what they saw last night.

"Man, I'm not sure what it was," Robb replied. He looked at the man asking the question. "What's it to you anyway?"

The man looked a little agitated that these two who were not being more cooperative. He grabbed a couple of drinking glasses from the stand next to the table where they were sitting. He placed an empty glass in front of each of them and then started to pour water into them from the pitcher sitting on the same stand.

"Here, take this," he said as he handed each a pill. "This will help with the headache."

He put the bottle of pills back in his jacket pocket.

The two looked at each other to see if the other one was going to take the pill or not. Then they both swallowed it down at the same time as they followed it with a drink of water.

"There now," the man said as he reached inside his jacket and pulled out a folded piece of paper. "Tell me if this is the creature that you encountered last night."

He unfolded the piece of paper that contained a sketch of VoLt.

The two men leaned forward to see the sketch and then immediately sat quickly back in their chairs.

"Yep, that's him," Chet answered nervously as he started to have flashbacks from the previous night.

Robb leaned forward and placed his hand on the table and asked in a low voice, "What is it?"

The man took the piece of paper and refolded it before placing it back inside his jacket.

"An old acquaintance," he answered.

"Must be," Robb answered as he studied the old piece of paper as the man placed it back in his pocket. "That looks like an old sketch. Whatever it is, it looked the same as that last night," he added.

Robb suddenly felt a little woozy and looked over at Chet, who was already passed out. He looked frantically back at the gentleman across the table from him.

"What did you…?" Robb uttered before he passed out from the effects of the drug.

He fell limp in his chair. The gentleman then stood up and opened his briefcase. He pulled out what looked like two dog collars. He placed one around each of their necks. They were fairly loose, but that was expected. On the back of the collar was a lock that he secured with a special pin key. He then walked back to his briefcase and pulled out a syringe, which contained a reddish chemical.

First he went to Chet, found a good vein in his arm, and injected him with the chemical. Then he proceeded to do the same to Robb. He calmly walked back to his briefcase, placed the syringe back, and pulled out a remote control device. He stood behind the table and pressed a button.

The button caused an electric shock to be delivered to the two collars. Both men shot up in their seats and instantly grabbed for their necks in pain, finding the collars hanging around their necks.

"What's the deal, man?" yelled Robb as he looked angrily at the man standing on the other side of the table. Chet was in too much shock to say anything.

"Who are you?" Robb yelled the question.

The man straightened his coat and proudly answered, "Who am I? I'm Professor Zen, and I'm your new master."

Then the professor pressed another button, which again shocked the two young men. As they winced in pain, their bodies began to transform. Their noses and jaws began to protrude from their faces, and they grew fangs from their teeth. Their arms, legs, and chest started to swell with new muscles. They began growling like dogs as they looked around, trying to fathom what was happening to them.

"What have you done to us?" growled the newly transformed Robb.

Zen smirked and replied, "I simply made you two useful for once in your life."

An officer stood guard outside the room. He couldn't see through the frosted window, but he could hear the loud roars of what he thought was general yelling between the counselor and his clients.

Then suddenly, the door violently swung open, catching the officer off guard. The door hit him with enough force to cause him to lose consciousness and fall to the floor. Then a chair from the room came flying out the door and crashed into a window across the hall, which shattered into pieces.

Several officers and clerks started coming out into the hallway to see what caused the sudden commotion. One of the creatures leaped out into the hallway and growled at the onlookers then jumped out the window and landed somewhere on the ground below. The second creature soon appeared as he growled at the remaining officers who were trying to get over the shock of suddenly seeing monster-like creatures running amuck in their building. It quickly followed the other one out the window.

Professor Zen casually walked out of the room. Then he tipped his Fedora to an officer to communicate his departure.

"What are those things?" asked a policeman, too frightened to move.

Zen climbed on the windowsill and answered, "Those are my pets. I call them Kronogs."

Then he jumped out the window only to be caught by his dog-like creatures. Then the three of them quickly disappeared into the darkness of the night.

CHAPTER 33

The markets opened at seven o'clock in the morning, and Miss Parsons generally liked to shop early on Tuesday, a routine of hers. She finished her cup of coffee and placed it in the sink to wash later. She put on her coat and grabbed her purse as she headed to the market. She opened the door only to find three men standing there.

"Oh my!" she said, startled, as she attempted to smile to cover up her embarrassment. "I'm sorry. Can I help you?" she said as she looked the gentleman in the face. Then a sudden fear came over her.

"Heading to the market, Miss Parsons?" the man asked.

Jessica tried to catch her breath while placing her hand over her heart in an attempt to calm herself down. "I'm sorry, do I know you?" she stammered.

"You should know me! Your old boyfriend has been a thorn in my side for over sixty years," the man said in an agitated tone as Jessica nervously shook her head no.

The man grabbed her by the wrist. "Now if memory serves, I had a deal with him to stay away," he said angrily. "Now it appears he has returned, and a deal is a deal."

"Oh no," she said as she quickly recalled Tim's last warning to her all those years ago. "Zen!" She gasped, then she tried to scream, but she couldn't find her breath.

Zen's new associates, Chet and Robb, were standing by to assist the professor.

"Don't fight him, ma'am. He means business," Chet said as he rubbed his neck where his collar hung.

"It looks like we have some catching up to do," Zen said as he escorted her down the hallway, out of the building, and into a waiting car.

Dustin had a standing appointment with the head pastor every Tuesday morning at nine o'clock. He reached the pastor's office and knocked on the door.

"Come in," the pastor said as he answered the knock.

"Morning, sir," Dustin said as he entered the room.

The pastor stood in front of his small television, watching a news report. He didn't even bother to lift his head to acknowledge Dustin's entrance. The pastor appeared to be fixated on the breaking news.

"Morning, Dustin," the pastor said, again without facing Dustin. "Have you heard about this?" the pastor asked as he finally looked at Dustin as he spoke.

"Uh, no," he replied as he stepped closer to the television to hear the news report.

Dustin's blood turned cold when he heard about the two creatures being caught on videotape coming out of nowhere at the police station. Then the video showed a tall, slender man who reportedly accompanied the creatures. A witness told the reporter that the gentleman informed him that the creatures were his pets and that he called them Kronogs.

"When did they start reporting this?" Dustin asked.

"Around five o'clock this morning. They've been showing it all morning," the pastor answered. "I just can't get over the footage of these so-called Kronogs. I've never seen anything like this."

They watched the end of the report before it started back over.

"Okay, back to business," the pastor said as he tried to steer away from the extraordinary events that had just occurred late the night before.

The two discussed the current concerns regarding the youth and ways to expand the ministry. Dustin had difficulty focusing on the meeting as his mind had been transfixed on the news report. The meeting lasted a little over an hour, and Dustin excused himself to go and tend to his routine church duties.

He entered the sanctuary and started heading for the back main doors when he recognized a familiar person sitting towards the back of the pews. He approached the figure and had a hard time believing who actually now stood before him.

"Brother Tim?" Dustin said with disbelief in his voice. "What brings you here?"

Tim had a very concerned yet agitated look on his face, much like a disappointed parent of a rule-breaking child.

"I read a news article yesterday about someone I believe we both know, which sparked my concern," he said.

Tim swallowed hard as he tried to continue, and Dustin saw Tim's face turn pale white.

"But then I saw the news this morning about the events at a police station last night." His hands began to shake as he continued. "Now I believe now my worst fears have come true, and I fear the worst for Jessica."

Dustin felt a little confused. He knew the newspaper article had brought some early, unwanted attention to his new alter ego, but he wasn't sure why the appearance of the dog-like creatures would have an effect on Jessica.

"You mean these Kronogs?" Dustin asked cautiously.

"No!" Tim answered angrily. "I mean the man that was with them in the video footage!"

"Who is it?" Dustin asked.

"It's Zen," Tim answered as a sudden drain of strength came over his face and body as he held on to the pew with all his might.

"How can that be? Wouldn't he have to be, like, a hundred years old now?" Dustin asked.

"Yes," Tim answered.

"Well, I don't understand," Dustin again said in complete confusion.

"Somehow, someway, he's managed to find a way to keep from aging," Tim answered.

The two sat in silence for a moment when the warning that Zen gave Tim nearly sixty-five years ago began to resonate in Dustin's head.

"We better check on Jessica," Dustin said.

The two men approached the senior citizen housing complex.

"How long has she lived here?" Tim asked as he tried to imagine how Jessica's life turned out.

"I don't know for sure," Dustin answered as they entered the unit where Jessica resided.

They located her door and knocked. Tim breathed heavily with anticipation of seeing her face again after all these years, but no one came to the door. Dustin knocked again. Concern came over both of them as their knocks went unanswered. Dustin stood silent as he strained to hear anything inside while Tim reached up and felt the top of the doorframe. He felt around for a moment and then brought his hand down, holding a key.

"Some things never change," Tim said with a small, subtle smile.

Using the key, they opened the door.

"Miss Parsons?" Dustin called out as he slowly opened the door. "Miss Parsons, are you here?"

There was no response.

Dustin cautiously checked the apartment for her. She was nowhere to be found. As Dustin reentered the living room, he asked, "Maybe she's at the market."

Tim stood there still by the front door. "I doubt it," Tim answered.

Dustin then noticed that Tim was holding Jessica's purse.

"It was lying here on the floor next to the door," Tim said solemnly.

Tim looked around Jessica's apartment. Guilt consumed his face.

Tim looked down and said, "Zen has her."

CHAPTER 34

Clouds started to cover the city as Dustin and Tim ran back to the Berthel Church. Dustin was surprised at how well Tim managed to keep up with him for being eighty-seven years old. He wondered if the formula that ran through Tim's body somehow was responsible for the great shape he appeared to be in. They reached the church and ran up the stairs and entered the large, front doors.

As they entered the sanctuary, the two winded men were met by the pastor.

"Is everything all right, Dustin?" the pastor asked with genuine concern.

"Honestly, sir, I don't know yet," Dustin paused to catch his breath as he attempted to introduce Tim to him. "Pastor Phillips, this is Tim Warner. He is an old acquaintance from Jennings," Dustin said as he slightly bent over with his hands on his hips.

Pastor Phillips held out his hand to greet him. Tim looked humbled as they shook hands.

"Pastor Phillips," Tim said as he shook the pastor hand. "Nice to meet you. I used to serve here as a youth minister in the early nineteen-forties."

"You must have worked with my grandfather," Phillips said.

"Excuse me?" Tim asked in return.

The reverend returned the puzzled look to Tim and answered, "Yes, my grandfather was Pastor Canow." Pastor Phillips paused for a second, and then his eyes lit up suddenly. "Of course, Tim Warner!"

Tim tried to catch his breath. The creases in his forehead indicated the pieces were coming together in his mind.

"I can't believe it took me this long to make the connection between Mr. Warner, the old attendant in Dustin's quarters, and the man that served with my grandfather all those years ago."

Dustin and Tim looked at each other in bewilderment.

"My grandfather said you had so much potential to really make an impact on the community," Pastor Phillips said.

Tim looked at him cautiously as if wondering just what kind of potential he referred to. Dustin gently interrupted the conversation, as more important issues were at hand.

"I'm sorry, but if you don't mind, I need to excuse myself," Dustin said as he headed toward his quarters, leaving Tim with Pastor Phillips as they continued to converse.

Dustin quickly made his way to his room and closed the door behind him. Then he pulled the dresser back, revealing the hidden door. He opened the door, reached in, and grabbed his black cloak and black sweatpants. He quickly changed into the old, black uniform and began to reach for the medallion when someone knocked on his door.

Dustin slowly cracked the door open to see who it could be. He wasn't surprise to see Tim standing there. He quickly opened it and allowed Tim in. Tim slowly entered as memories of the room quickly filled his mind.

He slightly raised his eyebrows and said, "It hasn't changed much."

Dustin glanced over the room and said, "I'm not really an interior decorator."

Then the two quickly refocused on the job at hand.

"Any plans?" Dustin asked of his old mentor.

Tim pulled out a scarf of Jessica's that he took from her apartment.

"You'll have to go back to her apartment and see if you can pick up the trail of her scent," he told Dustin as he handed him the scarf.

Dustin placed it in his inner cloak pocket where he kept the medallion. As soon as he touched the gold medallion, he began the transformation process. Tim stood in awe as he watched Dustin change into VoLt before his eyes.

"What about you?" the newly formed VoLt growled toward Tim.

"I'll play it by ear for now," Tim responded. "I'll be praying for you and Jessica."

VoLt nodded his head and said, "Thank you."

Then he disappeared into the tunnel's darkness. Tim closed the small door and pushed the dresser back in place then turned and knelt at Dustin's bed and began to pray.

CHAPTER 35

The underground train came rushing by. VoLt had readied himself, preparing to pounce on the train as the end neared. Then he leaped and landed on top of the train, quickly grabbing with his claws and adjusting to minimize the rocking back and forth of the train. This turned out to be a better landing than his first outing, and he hoped this was a sign that he would be able to find Jessica this easily.

He rode the underground train and leaped off just before it arrived at the next station. VoLt landed, having to use both legs and arms to land safely. Then he traveled down the sewer ways until he found himself right underneath the senior citizen housing complex. VoLt looked through the street sewer grates and found a grate that would likely not be seen by others in the area. He cautiously crawled out and quickly ran to Jessica's window. VoLt pulled out the scarf and sniffed it then held his head up and smelt the open air.

"There it is," VoLt said to himself, astonished.

VoLt climbed to the roof of the complex as he tried to determine the path the scent took. He knew it would be a challenge to track Jessica and not be seen. VoLt hated to admit it, but it would have to wait until dark.

In the spotless, dark laboratory came a knock on the door.

"Ah, right on time!" Professor Zen said as his appointment arrived. He opened the door and held himself proudly as he welcomed his guests. "Good evening, gentlemen. Come right on in."

The three men nodded as they entered in the laboratory. The men were of Middle Eastern descent and dressed in expensive, tailor-made suits. Zen looked over them as if trying to decide their country of origin. Then he waved off the curiosity, due mainly to the fact that he really didn't care. Zen only had one concern at this moment.

"I trust you made it here safely?" Zen asked.

"You mean, were we followed?" one of the men said.

"Well that too," Zen answered.

"Everything went well," another one of the men said.

"Well, let's get started, shall we?" Zen stated as business was about to begin.

The three men followed the professor across the room towards the back, south corner of the laboratory. There in front of them appeared to be a chamber. The professor proudly escorted the gentlemen completely around the dark-gray, steel structure. One side of the chamber had a control panel complete with keyboard, monitor, and numerous gauges.

"What is this?" asked the leader of the group.

Zen paused for a moment seemingly letting the words sink in. The look on his face indicated that he had been waiting for a long time to have someone ask him of his own marvelous invention.

"I'm sorry, I didn't catch your name?" Zen asked of the man.

"My apologies. My name is Mr. Gustav," he answered. "And these are my fellow associates, Mr. Mustavich and Mr. Pulmava."

Each man nodded their head as he was introduced.

Professor Zen then took his place proudly by the control panel of the chamber and began explaining his invention.

"Back in the late seventies and early eighties, when the world powers were focused on using nuclear power to build weapons to destroy each other, I began researching other possibilities for nuclear energy." He paused as he turned to marvel at his creation. "It took years and, unfortunately, several assistants to find a way to beat the human clock."

The three men stared suspiciously at the professor as he spoke.

"During my research, I discovered that certain exposure to human cells actually stopped the cell from aging. Then eventually, I was able to discover a way to turn back the clock on human aging altogether."

He paused again as he rubbed his chin with his right hand while holding his right elbow with his left and at his side.

"Needless to say, there was some 'collateral damage,' but as they say, all in the name of science."

Zen appeared to be recalling some of the associates he had lost due to his experiments.

"Finally, I was able to find a way to manipulate the nuclear energy, contain it, and expose a human being to it successfully."

The three men began to look at each other, wondering if this could really be true.

"Gentlemen, I understand that the person that sent you to me is in dire need of an invention such as this," Zen said with a raised eyebrow, indicating he knew the mastermind behind their organization.

"How do we know it works?" asked Mr. Mustavich.

"Well, my friends, I am a hundred and ten years old," Zen proudly announced.

"How do we know that?" Mr. Mustavich again asked.

"I understand your skepticism, that's why I have arranged a demonstration for you," the professor said as he began preparing the machine for exhibition.

"If this truly does work, why not patent it and have more created so that others can benefit from this?" asked Mr. Gustav.

"I built this for my own benefit—survival of the fittest at its finest. The only reason why I'm willing to part with it is because an old project has resurfaced that I would like to pursue again. And unfortunately, it requires finances that I currently do not have. That's why I'm selling this to the highest bidder," Professor Zen said as he explained himself.

None of the men responded, which Zen took as an acceptance of his business proposal.

"Now if you'll excuse me for a moment," Zen said as he walked around to the edge of the chamber.

He motioned to Chet and Robb, who were standing quietly next to a door.

Mr. Pulmava looked a little surprised that he didn't see the two men standing back there in the corner. Chet and Robb nodded to Zen as they opened the door and walked in. Then they soon came out, escorting Miss Parsons out of the room.

"Ah, Miss Parsons," Zen said as he faked a pleasant tone with Jessica. "Right this way."

The three perspective buyers appeared to be a little uneasy with the thought of sacrificing an elderly woman.

"Excuse me, Mr. Zen, I don't think this will be necessary," Mr. Gustav said as he expressed concern for the woman.

The three men looked at one another as they tried to justify the sacrifice.

"Remember, this is all for Allah," Mr. Pulmava said as he leaned into Gustav's shoulder to remind him.

Mr. Gustav paused for a moment and then nodded to Zen. "You may proceed."

The professor escorted Jessica inside the chamber and strapped her to a gurney. The chamber was constructed in steel, inside and out. There were small, vent-like holes throughout the inside of the chamber. There was a small, rectangular window that appeared to be at least six inches thick, which would match the rest of the thickness of the structure. On the opposite side of the chamber entry door was a small, cabinet-like door where Zen had the cylinders that contained the nuclear energy to power the structure.

As he strapped Jessica down, he leaned down to her and said, "Don't worry, it will only sting for a moment."

Then he stood up, gave her an evil smirk, and walked out the reinforced, lead door and locked it. Jessica didn't say anything. She just lay there with her eyes closed, appearing to be praying, expecting the worse.

Zen excitedly walked around to the front where the control panel resided and announced, "Shall we begin?"

Zen started working away at the control panel as the gauges began to react.

"If you like, gentlemen, you can witness the transformation on the other side," he said as he had to raise his voice a little over the hum of the machine.

The three men peered inside the window and were astonished at what they were seeing. Professor Zen monitored the levels of radiation that entered the chamber then worked away again on the keyboards to start the other stages of the process. He could monitor Jessica's vital signs and even see when the nuclear energy would drain her of life in some of the stages.

After several minutes, the readouts indicated that the procedure had been completed. Zen stood straight up and walked around to where his clients stood.

"Well, gentleman, do we have a deal?"

The three men had difficultly pulling themselves away from the window. Mr. Gustav tapped Mr. Pulmava on the shoulder as a sign to pay Zen for the invention. Mr. Pulmava walked over and handed Zen the briefcase of money. The professor quickly opened the briefcase to see and count the money. He then smiled and closed the briefcase.

"It has been a pleasure doing business with you. You may take the fusion of youth whenever you wish."

Zen turned around and began walking away when suddenly he found himself flying through the air and slammed against one of the laboratory walls. He fell to the ground and only lay there for a moment before being lifted again by a large hand gripping his shirt.

"Professor Zen, I presume," growled a large, dark-haired creature wearing a gold *V* medallion.

Zen tried to focus. He realized he was in VoLt's grasp but soon began to recognize that it was not the same creature that he knew.

"What? Who are you?" Zen asked as he winced in pain.

VoLt didn't answer. Instead he veered back with his fist and landed a hard punch against Zen's jaw, which sent him falling and rolling over on the right side. Zen rolled over onto his knees and appeared to be begging for mercy.

"You're not the VoLt I know. The other one had mercy," Zen said as he pleaded to be spared.

"Mercy?" VoLt responded. "You may have God's mercy, but you do not have mine!"

VoLt reached down and picked him up again and glared into Zen's eyes.

"What did you do to Miss Parsons?" he growled as the followed the question with a head butt to Zen's forehead. Then he threw Zen to the ground.

VoLt looked up to see the three Muslim men staring at him in shock. The three men then looked down at the briefcase of money that lay on the ground between them. VoLt stared them down and gestured with his hand as if daring them to come and get the briefcase. Mr. Pulmava took a step forward to only be met back with a large step by the creature. The three men then retreated and bolted for the door without the briefcase.

The creature walked over to where the briefcase rested, and while he had his back to Zen, the professor managed to muster the strength to pull out a remote control device and push a green button. Instantly, Robb and Chet, who were hiding from the creature, began the transforming process into the Kronogs.

"Get him!" Zen shouted.

The Kronogs reacted instantly, as they were programmed to respond to whatever command they received.

VoLt looked up to see the two creatures advance towards him quickly from both sides. He crouched down in a defensive stance as the two creatures attacked at the same time. The Kronogs' claws dug into VoLt's chest and arms as they tried to rip him apart. VoLt violently began fighting off the attackers. He managed to throw one Kronog off by grabbing it by the neck and throwing him. Then VoLt focused his attention on the other creature and grabbed him by his hair, spinning around and flinging the creature like a rag doll.

VoLt stood with his back to the large laboratory window that overlooked the river flowing by nearly twenty-five feet below. The two Kronogs quickly recovered and once again stood in attack position on each side of VoLt. Zen, who by now had managed to stand up, wiped the blood from his mouth shouted another command. "Attack!"

The Kronogs then lunged and attacked VoLt. The force and the weight of the three caused them to fall back and crash through window and land in the river below.

The three plunged nearly ten feet into the water before they were able to resurface. The two Kronogs quickly tried to paddle their way back to the shore as VoLt stayed submerged and attacked his adversaries from under the water by pulling them back under where they were not able to defend themselves. VoLt then reached the shoreline as he waited for them to crawl out.

Professor Zen stood far above them, watching the three battle in the river below. Disgusted with the performance of his Kronogs, he turned around to retrieve his briefcase and escape. Instead, he was met by the elder VoLt, who held the briefcase.

Zen stood in shock as the elder VoLt asked, "Looking for this?" He swung the briefcase upward, slamming it against Zen's lower chin.

The professor rolled over on his side as he quickly tried to regain his stability and focus on what had just attacked him. Before him stood the same creature that he had encountered nearly sixty-five years before, only gray streaks ran through what used to be his brown mane. The rest of the elder VoLt's physique hid under an old, green military poncho. Zen scrambled to his feet, using the wall behind him for support as he tried to grapple with what he saw.

"How…how can there be two of you?" Zen asked.

Zen looked for the hardware around VoLt's neck and didn't see anything but soon recognized the silver bracelets around VoLt's wrists.

The elder VoLt walked over to him and grabbed Zen by the chest and lifted the professor up to his face. Without addressing Zen's question, VoLt looked squarely into his eyes and asked in an angry growl, "Where is Jessica?"

Zen found himself at a loss for words but glanced over at the chamber where Jessica was located. VoLt turned to look at the chamber, and fearing the worse, he threw the professor violently across the room. The professor landed on a table, causing it to collapse along with all the contents and shelves around it. Zen didn't move.

VoLt ran to the chamber and unlocked the reinforced door with a noticeable clank. He opened it and found Jessica lying on the table. Her eyes were closed, but she appeared to be squinting her eyes shut as if anticipating something painful to come at her.

It took him only a second to recognize her. She looked the exact same way as she did when he left all those years ago. Amazement covered his face, trying to understand how Zen managed to do this. His hands quivered as he longed to hold her again. VoLt slowly approached and leaned over her.

"Jessica, it's me."

She opened her eyes and saw her old hero standing over her. Tears welled up in her eyes as she said, "It's you!"

VoLt quickly loosened the straps that were holding Jessica to the table. As soon as she was free, she immediately sat up and embraced him.

"Oh, thank you, Lord!" she prayed out.

VoLt returned the embrace as he too thanked God for the chance to see and hold her once again.

Jessica pulled away to look at him and said, "Can we get out of here?"

VoLt smiled and picked her up and carried her out of the chamber.

"Where's Zen?" Jessica asked as she quickly looked around for him.

VoLt just pointed to the pile where Zen lay amongst the broken table, shelving, and equipment.

"Is he dead?" she asked, hoping for a confirmation.

"I don't know," VoLt said with a hint of remorse.

Then VoLt took off the bracelets that triggered his transformation and threw them aside. They were the same bracelets that Charles had used to transform into Evilution all those years before. He had taken them off of Charles the night he died and had kept them hidden. Jessica watched the creature transform back into Tim. He stood there, almost embarrassed over his appearance. He was no longer the young man that she last seen all those years ago.

He smiled at her and said, "Well, it's good to see that you have aged so well."

Jessica seemed to pick up the hint of jealously from him, but her expression indicated she didn't know what he meant exactly.

"What's that supposed to mean, Tim Warner?" she asked with her hands on her hips and smiling in a mischievous way. "I know I'm not exactly a spring chicken anymore, but—"

Tim interrupted her as he pointed to a mirror behind them. She turned around and became overwhelmed with shock that she was not the eighty-something-year-old woman anymore. Instead she looked like a twenty-five-year-old woman again.

"What in heaven's name?" she mumbled as she softly touched the side of her cheek. She couldn't believe her eyes. Gone were the wrinkles in her face; gone were the long strands of gray hair, and in its place was soft, young skin and long, light-brown hair.

"Zen discovered a way to turn back the human clock," Tim said as he gestured to the chamber that she had just come from.

Jessica looked at Tim and embraced him.

"I don't care! I'm just glad to be with you again."

Finally, after all these years apart, they were together at last. They held each other the same as they had all those years ago. He gently rubbed his hands up and down her back with astonishment on his face that he was actually holding her again. She held him tight. She gently shook her head as if trying not to think about the wasted years that were taken from them. She wanted those years back.

She grabbed Tim's arms and pulled back to look at him face-to-face, "Maybe the same thing can happen to—"

She was interrupted by an unexpected forceful push coming from Tim's back, which sent them both falling to the ground.

Tim winced in pain, holding his back while lying on the ground. Jessica looked up to see Professor Zen standing over the two of them with a steel rod in his hands. He struck Tim by swinging the rod like a baseball bat to Tim's back. Zen stood over him, both hands clinching the steel post, in attack position. Then Zen glanced down on the ground and saw the metal bracelets. As if finding a buried treasure, Zen eyes gleamed as he realized the hardware that he had desperately searched for now appeared to be within his reach—the bracelets of Evilution.

The professor dropped the rod with a loud, rumbling, rattling clank on the concrete floor, as he took a gamble that he no longer needed the steel rod for the advantage over his two rivals. He reached down and grabbed the bracelets, which instantly had an effect over his body. Tim and Jessica watched in horror as they witnessed Zen begin to transform right before their eyes. The clothing began to rip at the seams, only to unveil the impressive, muscular physique that began to form. A rapid burst of blond hair covered his chest and arms, followed by the beautiful, flowing mane that grew from his head and neck. At long last, Professor Zen had finally acquired the ability he had searched for—a search that spanned over sixty-five years. The creature known as Evilution stared at his reflection in the mirror next to the steal chamber and then let out a frightening, growling laughter that filled the laboratory.

CHAPTER 36

Standing on the shore, VoLt waited for the Kronogs to emerge from the river. They resurfaced as they slowly paddled to where they could stand. VoLt prepared himself as he glanced back and forth between the two creatures. Then one of them leaped at VoLt, but he caught it in midair and flipped it over his shoulder, causing the creature to land on its back on the rocky shore. But as he finished fighting off that creature, the other Kronog attacked. It lunged at VoLt's chest, causing him to fall on his back. Pain shot through VoLt when the Kronog pounced on his chest as it delivered punches, one after the other.

The anger grew in VoLt with each and every punch he received. The animal then delivered a ferocious blow that caused him to roll over on his left side. Despite the intense, stinging agony, VoLt managed to free up his right arm and quickly return the punch with a swing of his own that resulted with the creature being forced off as it yelped in pain.

VoLt stood up facing the animal as it lay wincing, only to be attacked from the other one from behind. The creature's claws dug into Volt's shoulder blades, ripping through his cloak. VoLt growled in agony as he arched his back. He reached back and managed to grab the Kronog and fling it over his head, with the creature landing on its side.

Before the Kronog could get up, VoLt walked over and grabbed him by the neck with his right arm and lifted him up. That's when he saw the collar around its neck. He reached with his left hand and ripped the collar off. Instantly, the animal turned back into Chet.

"You!" VoLt yelled with anger at recognizing the same individual that he had already encountered two other times. Shame momentarily ran through VoLt's senses that he had let this thug slip through his cleansing clutch on the previous occasions.

Chet looked at VoLt with fear in his eyes and begged for mercy. "Please don't kill me! I had no control!"

VoLt glared into his eyes and could tell he was telling the truth but could still see a lot of the evil glow in his eyes. He lowered Chet to the ground and placed his hand over Chet's face.

"Repent!" VoLt growled.

Suddenly, the evilness left Chet only to be consumed by VoLt. Chet dropped to the ground after the cleansing and began to weep. VoLt then turned his attention to the other creature and walked over to it. He reached down and ripped off the collar, allowing the Kronog to transform back into Robb.

Robb slowly came to only to find himself eye-to-eye with the vigilante creature as VoLt placed his hand over Robb's face.

"Repent!" VoLt growled.

Once again, the evil that consumed Robb drained into VoLt as he miraculously took it in. Then the creature stood up straight and spewed the hot, burning bile from his mouth. He took out a match; knelt down; struck it against a rock, igniting it; and dropped the match on the bile.

The disgusting fluid erupted into a purple fireball along with an evil hiss that burned out in just seconds. VoLt looked over at Chet and Robb, who both were still lying on the ground, visibly shaken by the sudden release of wrongdoing that had controlled their lives for so long.

"Turn yourself in. If you don't, I will hunt you down," VoLt barked.

Chet and Robb looked at each other and nodded their heads in agreement nervously, knowing full well that VoLt would be true to his word.

Evilution held Tim by the chest as he smiled a sinister smile.

"Now, you're about to see what it feels like being at the other end of this spectrum."

Evilution threw Tim against the wall as Tim winced in pain. Tim reached around his back in an attempt to stop the throbbing soreness as he watched Evilution approach him and delivered a backhanded blow to his jaw, which snapped his head back as blood sprayed from his mouth.

"No!" Jessica shouted.

Evilution paused to look over at Jessica and muttered, "Don't worry, you're next."

Then he turned his attention back to Tim, only to be met by a blow to his head by a steel rod that Tim delivered.

Evilution staggered back a couple of feet as Tim took another swing to Evilution's left side. The creature cringed in pain as Tim delivered another blow to the creature's backside. Arching his back in agony, Tim took the rod and placed it under Evilution's chin and forced the creature to look up at him. This act enraged Evilution, as it appeared to be a demeaning insult. The creature grabbed the end of the rod from under his chin and shoved it back toward Tim. The force that he put into it caused the rod to slip through Tim's hand, ripping through the poncho and puncturing his chest.

"Tim!" Jessica screamed in horror.

Tim staggered back and forth as he tried to pull the rod from his torso. Then the creature walked over and grabbed the end of the rod and said, "Allow me," yanking the rod out of Tim's chest.

The younger VoLt entered the laboratory just as Evilution pulled the rod out of Tim.

"No!" he roared as he quickly leaped in the air with Evilution his target.

Evilution turned in time to feel the brunt force of VoLt's hands pound against his chest. Evilution stammered backward as he tried to shake off the pain from VoLt's thunderous shove, but before he could gain back his balance, VoLt struck again. This time, the savage beast landed a right fist against his left jaw, which was immediately followed by a left fist to his right jaw. Evilution tried desperately to hold on to his consciousness.

The rage that flowed through VoLt was nothing like he had ever worked with before. He could almost feel himself losing control of his actions, as if something else had taken over. As he watched Evilution stagger with his feet, he knew he had to end this war. Evilution staggered around in a circle, leaving his back to VoLt. That is when VoLt lunged at Evilution's back, causing him to land hard on the floor face-first. VoLt then took Evilution's right arm and pulled it behind him and yanked off one of the bracelets. Then he grabbed the left arm and removed that bracelet as well. Instantly, the creature transformed back into Professor Zen. VoLt then placed the bracelets in his inner cloak pocket.

VoLt reached over and yanked Zen up by his shredded clothes.

"It's over, Zen!" he said as he shoved the professor against the wall with enough force that Zen's head snapped back, hitting the wall with a painful thud. Zen then fell to the ground, curled up in a fetal ball.

VoLt reached for a pocket inside his cloak. He pulled out the collars that he tore of the Kronogs. He took the collars and said, "By the way, I believe these are yours," as he dropped them at Zen's feet.

"As they say, their bark was worse than their bite."

VoLt looked over to see Jessica tending to Tim. Tears streamed down her face as she tried to comfort him. VoLt ran over to Jessica and Tim and knelt down beside them. Jessica tried to stop the bleeding as much as she could, but the wound was too severe.

"We had a deal," Zen said in a winced voice as he watched the two of them tend to Tim. "He broke his end of the deal, so I had to break him."

Zen tried to sit up, trying to mask the pain he was obviously in.

Tim looked at the professor, and with blood seeping out of his mouth, he softly asked, "How?"

Knowing what he meant, Zen answered. "Oh, how did I obtain the ability to transform?"

In a conceited tone, Zen began to explain as he managed to stand, leaning against the wall.

"That's easy. Once Charles returned to me as Evilution, I was intrigued, to say the least, about his new powers. Knowing that he so selfishly took all the formula, I had to come up with a way to obtain the power myself. So naturally, I requested a sample of his blood to study. I took a full syringe of his blood to examine and simply injected myself with the remnants of Charles's plasma. From then, my plan was to take the bracelets from him when the moment presented itself. Instead, you managed to steal them when you killed Charles."

"I didn't kill him!" Tim said, gasping for strength.

"VoLt," Jessica cried softly, "he's losing a lot of blood." She continued to press down hard on Tim's injury.

VoLt stared down at Zen; he swallowed hard and asked, "Can your machine help him?"

Zen didn't answer. He just sat there stewing over his situation. Frustrated, VoLt barked the question again, "I asked, can your machine help him?"

Zen jerked his head to glare back at Tim. "I suppose it could."

"Then I suppose you will help him!" VoLt replied as he yanked Zen from leaning against the wall.

VoLt dragged him over to where Tim and Jessica were lying on the floor. While holding Zen firmly by his upper arm with one hand, he leaned over to help Jessica with getting Tim up on his feet. They managed to enter the chamber were VoLt and Jessica laid Tim on the table.

"Now what?" VoLt asked of Zen.

"I have to make a slight modification to the power lines inside this panel," Zen said as he pointed to the small door at the opposite side of the chamber entry door.

"Then do it!" VoLt ordered.

Zen opened the door, reached in, and yanked a tube that ran a coolant to the small nuclear reactor. Instantly, alarms started sounding as VoLt yelled at Zen.

"What did you do?"

"I simply leveled the playing field," Zen said as he turned around with a smirk to the other three.

VoLt stepped toward the small panel and shoved Zen aside, causing Zen to land headfirst against the steel wall, knocking him out cold. VoLt tried to place the tubing back in place. It partially worked as VoLt saw the gauges react to the tube being put back in place, but the gauges still indicated that the reactor was still in danger of meltdown.

"I can only slow it down," VoLt said as he tried to hold it with all his might.

"Jessica, you got to take Tim and get out of here!"

She looked with fear at VoLt as she asked, "What? What about you?"

VoLt turned back his attention to the damaged pipe. "Just go."

Jessica helped Tim up to his feet and tried to motion him out the door, but Tim wouldn't move.

"No," Tim said. "I'll stay and hold the line."

Jessica's tears began streaming down her face. "No, Tim, No!"

Tim tried to calm her down. "Jessica, it's my time. It's my turn."

Jessica frantically looked at him as if searching for other possible solutions.

VoLt looked at Tim and said, "Go, you two, now!"

Holding his hand to his chest, Tim walked over to VoLt and said, "Son, it's okay. They need you. It's your calling."

VoLt wanted to argue, but he knew time was running out, and if he didn't obey Tim, then more than likely none of them would survive. He bowed his head and prayed for Tim's soul as tears began streaming from his eyes.

"I'm sorry." It was all VoLt could say.

"It's okay," Tim said with a small smile.

"Jessica," Tim said. He called for her to come over to him. "Know that I always loved you. From the moment I first saw you, I loved you."

Jessica embraced him and replied, "I'll always love you."

VoLt watched them as they held each other for the last time. Reading the gauges, he knew she had to let go soon.

"Jessica," VoLt softly whispered.

"Okay, go," Tim said as he gently pushed Jessica away.

VoLt reluctantly bent down and picked up Zen and threw him over the shoulder and then turned to Tim as he stood in the doorway of the chamber. He nodded his head and said, "Thank you, and God bless you."

Tim nodded an acknowledgment as tears welled up in his eyes. "Take care of Jessica and yourself."

As they quickly left the laboratory, VoLt bent down and picked up the briefcase of money and handed it to Jessica for her to carry. They ran to the open, shattered window, where he picked Jessica up with his right arm while still having Zen flung over his left shoulder. Then he leaped out the window and landed two stories down on the sidewalk just below that ran along the river that VoLt had previously battled in. VoLt landed square and hard on his feet. Bolts of pain shot up his spine, but he fought through the intensity, letting Jessica down his side. As they started running for safety, VoLt looked down over the boardwalk to see both Chet and Robb still sitting there on the shore as if pondering their fates. They both looked at him in shock as they saw the two of them running from the building.

VoLt hollered, "If you want to live, you better follow us now!"

The two men didn't hesitate and quickly jumped to their feet and followed.

Tim held the pipeline with all his might, as the chamber's sirens became more intense. His hands appeared to become heavy and numb as they slowly started to lose their grip on the pipeline. His legs began to quiver as his eyes began to close. In his last moments of breath, the softly sang the chorus of one of his favorite hymns.

"It is well (it is well), with my soul…(with my soul), it is well, it is well, with my soul."

Then Tim allowed himself to be consumed with eternal peace.

CHAPTER 37

The old warehouse erupted into a large explosion. VoLt dropped the professor to the ground and quickly grabbed Jessica and covered her with his cloak. VoLt threw his hood up and cradled Jessica as the intense heat covered them. Despite the fact that had managed to run nearly three hundred feet from the warehouse where the laboratory had been, the explosion was extremely hot. Chet and Robb were curled up to protect their faces from the heat as Zen lay unprotected on the ground.

The radioactive blast completely destroyed the warehouse and the adjacent buildings. The five of them managed to escape from structural danger, but they were close enough to the fireball that it burned up the clean air they breathed, so much so that Chet and Robb passed out from the temporary lack of oxygen while Jessica and VoLt were protected by the cloak that Jessica had created for Tim all those years ago.

After a few moments, the heat began to subside, and Volt threw back his hood to test the air.

"I think it's safe now, Jessica," he said as he reached down to help her to her feet.

She didn't say anything. Her face was buried in her hands as VoLt could see her body quivering from an unexplainable heartbreak.

"Jessica, listen to me," he said as he knelt down beside her. "We're still not in the clear."

She tried to lift her head to hear, but the tears wouldn't stop flowing.

"Why?" was all that she could say.

VoLt didn't know if she was referring to why they had to keep moving or why Tim had to die. The pastor in him wanted to console her and pray with her, but the situation that they were in would not to allow for that.

"Jessica, you have to go home and—"

She interrupted him by finishing his sentence. "And pack your things."

She stood up with an obviously frustrated demeanor and said, "I'm familiar with the routine."

They could hear the sirens coming in the distance. VoLt looked off in the directions that they were coming from.

He turned back to her and said, "Then go to the church. I'll be there shortly." He paused and tried to look her in the eyes. "Jessica, I'm so sorry."

She didn't say anything but looked at Zen's unconscious body lying on the ground as if indicating he was the only one to blame. "I'll take care of him. Now go," he said as he placed his hand gently on her shoulder.

Minutes later, the fire trucks and police vehicles arrived at the scene of the explosion. VoLt stood on top of one of the buildings that managed to survive the blast. He scanned over the crowds of police, hoping to find an officer in charge. He eventually located a policeman that appeared to be commanding the situation.

"All right, I need to know the names of businesses that were located in this area," the police chief said. "I know most of these buildings were vacant, but I want to make sure that no one was here during this incident."

The officers scattered as they responded to orders to find possible victims. The police chief opened his door and reached for his radio inside when suddenly something smashed his car door window. The police chief smacked his head on the doorframe as he reacted to the shattering glass.

He quickly tried to regain his composure and began looking around for the cause of the broken window, all the while rubbing his head and trying to dull the throbbing pain.

He found a large rock lying among the broken glass. The chief quickly determined that it had come from behind him. He looked around and saw nobody. Then he began to look at the rooftops of the surrounding buildings.

Something caught his eye. He looked again and saw some type of figure standing on top of one of the buildings. He strained to look at the person, and then he realized that the figure was pointing toward a specific spot about fifty yards away. The police chief placed his hand on his gun as if reacting to his first instinct and arresting the dark figure, but instead he followed the figure's request and went in the direction he was pointing.

The officer quickly made his way over and looked down the retaining wall onto the riverbank below. To his surprise, lying unconscious, were the two suspects that had escaped nights ago along with the very man that caused the breakout. The police chief turned around to let the dark figure know that he found them, but the figure was gone.

VoLt made his way back to the secret tunnel that led him to his living quarters. He took off his medallion and quickly transformed back into Dustin. He opened the small, secret door and pushed the dresser aside to enter his room.

To his surprise, he found Jessica sitting on his bed while Pastor Phillips leaned against his desk. The pastor stood frozen in disbelief as he watched Dustin emerge from nowhere behind the dresser. Dustin stood silent in embarrassment as he searched for words to explain everything. He didn't know where to begin as he felt a cold sweat come over him.

"Dustin, what in the world is going on?" Phillips asked. "What are you doing coming from behind there?"

Dustin raised his eyebrows and opened his mouth, but nothing came out.

"This young woman insisted on waiting in your quarters until you got home," Phillips continued with a hint of agitation.

"Yes, well, uh," Dustin replied.

"He's VoLt," Jessica answered for him.

A blank look came over Dustin as he glanced over to Jessica as she abruptly announced his alter ego.

"VoLt?" the reverend asked. He paused. Then his eyes popped open wide. "As in the Vigilante of Lord's Treasures?"

"Yes," she replied.

"But I thought that was just an old urban legend that my grandfather used to talk about."

"It's real…I mean, he's real. I mean, it's me," Dustin said.

"So it's true?" Pastor Phillips asked Dustin. He raised his eyebrows in confusion.

Dustin nodded his head softly.

Phillips walked over to Dustin. "You're the new VoLt."

Dustin modestly ran his fingers through his hair.

"Yes, he is," Jessica said with a smile, despite the fact that her eyes were red and swollen from crying. She stood up and hugged Dustin as he returned the embrace.

Pastor Phillips still seemed confused. "And I'm sorry, you are?" he asked of the woman who held Dustin.

Dustin laughed lightly, "You might want to take a seat for this one, sir. This is Jessica."

The pastor was still confused. "Jessica who?" he asked.

Dustin smiled and answered, "Jessica Parsons."

Pastor Phillips looked at Jessica and suddenly realized he was indeed looking at a twenty-five-year-old Jessica.

"I think I will take that seat," he said as he sat down.

Dustin and Jessica proceeded to tell the pastor everything, including the loss of their dear friend.

Later in the evening, the three of them sat in the sanctuary discussing their next move. They knew Zen would use Jessica as a pawn to get what he wanted and with several million euros missing, it would just be a matter of time before hired mercenaries would come looking for Jessica. They had to protect her.

The main door at the back opened, and a gentleman walked in. Dustin stood up quickly, feeling caught off guard and still a little edgy.

Phillips walked by Dustin and placed his hand on his shoulder, "It's okay. He's a friend."

The man approached them, and Dustin and Jessica began to recognize his face as a fellow church member.

"Yes, sir, how can I help?" the man said as he shook the pastor's hand.

"First, thank you for coming." The pastor paused. "This is Detective Hobbs, and this is Dustin and Jessica."

"Sure, the youth director. Nice to finally meet you, and miss," he said as he nodded toward Jessica.

"Arnie, we have an issue," the pastor began to explain. "There are terrorists here in London that will be looking for her as well as the large sum of money that they left behind. We need to protect her. Do you have any suggestions?"

Officer Hobbs had known Pastor Phillips since they were teenagers themselves. Knowing the character of Phillips, he knew the situation had to be legitimate.

"How much money?" the detective asked.

"About five million euros," Dustin replied. "Five million euros of blood money. They were after the device that caused the explosion in the old warehouse district."

Hobbs scratched his head with intrigue, wanting desperately to find out more about this device, but the desperation on their faces told him that he would have to enquire about that more at a later time. Right now, he had a young woman to protect.

"Arnie, do you think you could help us?" Phillips asked.

With a small, confident smile, Hobbs replied, "Hey, I've been on the force for over fifteen years. I've been blessed with promotions and responsibilities. I can assure you we can get this situation taken care of."

The three let out a collective sigh of relief, realizing that they were in good hands.

"So, are we talking about relocating?" Detective Hobbs asked.

"I think so," Dustin replied.

The actual words were finally sinking in with Jessica as she took a deep breath with fearful anticipation of which direction her life was suddenly going to take.

"And maybe a new name?" Dustin added as he gave a small, regretful look to her.

"Ah, yes, a new identity," Detective Hobbs replied.

Jessica softly nodded her head in agreement.

"Well, maybe we can keep the money hidden from them. Make them come out into the light to look for it. We'll also stake out your residence. If they show up, we'll nab 'em," Hobbs said with a smile. "I'll get to work on it right away. I'll have the paperwork filled out tomorrow. Then I'll personally have it processed."

The detective pulled out a piece of paper to write down some specific information about Jessica.

"Okay, what name will I put down for you?" Hobbs asked.

Jessica looked at both Pastor Phillips and Dustin. "Is it okay to keep my first name?" she asked.

"Well, how about we change it a little? How do you feel about Jessie?" Hobbs asked.

She softly shook her head in agreement.

"Now, for a last name…"

Her voice cracked as she answered. "Warner. I want it to be Warner."

CHAPTER 38

The crowd slowly filled the sanctuary with church members and other acquaintances of Jessica Parsons and Tim Warner.

As Dustin and Pastor Phillips sat in front facing the congregation, Dustin made eye contact with Tim's niece, Maggie, as she made her way down to the third pew. He slightly nodded his head as she discretely gave a small wave back to him. Dustin couldn't help but feel guilty. If he never had found that gold watch along with the determination to find the rightful owner, Tim would still be alive.

Pastor Phillips began speaking eloquently about the lives of Jessica and Tim. He spoke of the years of service that they dedicated to the Lord. Then he spoke about their love for each other. Despite the fact that the time they spent together was only for a few short months, they stayed faithful to each other for the remainder of their lives.

Dustin casually scanned the audience to see if he could see her. He found her. She sat on the opposite side of the pew she normally sat. Her regular seat was ceremoniously left empty. They made eye contact, and he could tell by her eyes that she was pleased with the turnout for her own funeral, despite the pain still being fresh in her heart.

The service ended with a collection of Jessica and Tim's favorite hymns.

After the service, the crowds slowly dispersed. Jessica sat quietly as members of the church passed by her without even noticing her. She patiently sat as she watched Dustin greet and thank people for attending the service. She watched as he spoke with one of Tim's family members.

"Maggie, I can't express how sorry I am about our loss," Dustin began as he greeted Tim's niece.

"Thank you, Dustin," Maggie answered. "I'm just glad that he finally made contact with someone after all those years that seemed to answer the prayers that he had been pleading for. I don't know what brought you into Uncle Tim's life here at the end, but it made a big impact on him."

Dustin nodded his head in agreement as he fought back the sudden rush of tears. Then he noticed Maggie holding an old, leather journal.

"Is that your Uncle Tim's?" Dustin asked, pointing to the leather-bound book.

"Yes," she answered as she held it up with her left hand resting on top of it. "He left a note requesting me to give this to you if anything should happen to him."

Maggie bit her lip to keep her composure.

"I found it this morning as I sat in his room. He must of have known his time was near," she continued as she handed it over to Dustin. "I looked through it briefly. It's mainly entries of his life. A lot of it is during his service in World War II."

Dustin tenderly accepted the journal from Maggie and glanced over a couple of pages when a particular note caught his eye.

June 22, 1941—We were stationed in a little village in France. We earned some R/R. My comrades were taking a break from the fighting, but I couldn't get those images out of my head. I had to make what was wrong right. I took my *V* piece and made my way back to the village. Nazis were still bunkered down on the west side of town. There were five in the first bunker I visited...

Dustin's eyes widened as he began to realize the extent of Tim's service.

"I don't know what to say," Tim replied as he held the journal.

"You don't have to say anything," Maggie said. "I know we didn't get off on the right foot when you came up to visit, but I want you to know that my uncle seemed to be at true peace once you left. He finally began speaking fondly as he looked back over his life. The bitterness seemed to finally fade, and for that, I want to say thank you."

She reached in and gave Dustin a hug—a sharp contrast to their last meeting.

"Take care of yourself," she said as she pulled back.

"You too. If you need anything, don't hesitate to contact me," Dustin replied.

"Will do."

Maggie made her way to the back and left the church.

The crowd had nearly dispersed as Jessica waited patiently in the back of the church. She looked down in an attempt to cover up the smile as longtime friends passed by her without recognizing her. It noticeably helped ease the pain of losing Tim.

Dustin finally made his way over to Jessica.

"So, what did you think?" Dustin asked her of her own funeral service.

"Very nice. Very, very nice."

"Good."

"Who was that woman you were speaking to?" Jessica asked.

"That was Tim's niece, Maggie."

"Really? She seems very nice and sweet."

"Yeah," Dustin answered, knowing that Jessica must have been thinking that Maggie could have been her niece too if things would have worked out differently.

"We had a bit of a rough start, but it's okay now," Dustin said as he lightly weighed the journal with his hand in front of him. "He left this for me, but I want you to have it. If you come across anything that might benefit me, you can let me know."

"I can't," she said.

"No, I insist. You two were robbed of a life together. Now you can at least know the life he had."

"I don't know what to say."

She gently accepted the journal and caressed it softly.

"You don't have to say anything at all," Dustin replied as he gently rubbed her shoulder.

Teary eyed, Jessica looked over the church.

"There are a lot of memories here," she said.

"Yeah, I imagine there are," Dustin said. They stood there in silence as Jessica reminisced. She let out a deep sigh and tried to change the subject.

"So, you are sure you don't mind taking me to the airport tomorrow?" Jessica asked as she started to make her way to the door.

"No, not at all," Dustin responded as he walked beside her as they approached the door, his hands shoved in his pockets and eyes looking down on the floor as they walked.

"It may sound kind of funny, but I always enjoy going to the airport," he said.

"Oh really, why is that?" she inquired.

"Oh, just seeing all the people who are there. Some are there to pick up loved ones, some are there to say good-bye, while others are there due to business, others off to vacations." He paused. "Then there are the ones like you—off to an adventure to parts unknown," he said as he cocked his head to her and smiled.

"I just can't believe it," she said with a blank stare, looking past Dustin.

"Yeah, it is kind of wild," he responded. He paused for a moment, knowing how overwhelming the past few days had been.

"So you and Detective Hobbs were able to get everything planned?" Dustin asked.

"Yes, but I feel guilty using part of that blood money to fund my new life," Jessica said.

"Don't. It's easier to fund this expedition with money that nobody wants to claim right now. Besides, there's still plenty of money left to bring them back looking for it. Once they do, they will be dealt with," Dustin said.

Jessica looked at Dustin, knowing full well what he meant.

"So, Zen is still in police custody?" she asked, looking for confirmation that she was still safe for the moment.

"Yes," he answered. "They think they have enough evidence to connect Zen to the explosion and the death of

Tim and you," he added. "We don't know how long they'll be able to hold on to him though. He's a little bit on the sly side."

"But, Dustin, I'm not dead. How can they charge him with that?"

"I'm leaving that with Detective Hobbs, 'cause technically, Jessica Parsons does not exist anymore," Dustin replied, feeling a little uncomfortable about that too.

"I don't know. I feel that might stir him up that much more," she responded.

"Maybe that's the intention," Dustin said, shrugging his shoulders as if trying to understand it himself.

They approached Pastor Phillips as he greeted people leaving the church.

"Thank you, Reverend," Jessica said as he gave the pastor a hug. "It was beautiful."

"Well, thank you, Jessica," Pastor Phillips said as he looked around cautiously to make sure no one heard him call her by her name. "It's not every day that a person gets to listen to their own funeral. And besides, when the person you are speaking about is as sweet and genuine as you, it makes it a lot easier," the pastor added. "So, I guess you are off to new adventures?"

"Yes, I guess so," Jessica replied as she tried to brush off the compliment. "I just want to thank you for everything. Your family has been so good to me all these years."

She tried to fight back the tears.

"It's been an honor serving beside you," the pastor said. He shook her hand while placing his other hand on top of hers.

She excused herself and turned around one last time to look at the Berthel Church. She tried to burn one more mental picture of the church into her memory.

In a cold, lonely cell, Professor Zen lay on the cot, still nursing his sore, bruised body. His skin was still sore from the extreme heat that he was exposed to during the blast when he lay unconscious. He raised his left hand in front of him, looking at it, first looking at his palm and then turning it over and looking at the top. He made a fist, held it for a moment, and released it, only to make another fist again. A small smirk came across his face as if he felt something different running through his system.

A guard walked up and knocked on his cell door. Zen didn't move, appearing to ignore another taunt by a guard to keep him awake so he wouldn't find any comfort in sleeping. Then the guard knocked again, this time a little harder.

"Zen, you have a visitor," the guard barked.

The professor looked surprised as he tried to think who would come to see him. He slowly sat up and looked at the guard.

"Who is it?" Zen asked.

"I don't know," the guard answered in an annoyed tone. "Says he's your lawyer."

Raising an eyebrow, Zen slowly stood up from his bed and walked to the door. The guard opened the door and placed handcuffs on the professor. Zen winced slightly as the handcuffs were slapped on. The guard led him to the room where the professor found his lawyer seated.

Mr. Gustav stood up as the guard brought the professor into the room and sat him down.

"Mr. Gustav, what brings you by?" Zen asked of his visitor.

"Well, for starters, how about the two murder charges against you," Gustav replied as he acted out the part of his lawyer.

"Two?" Zen replied as he tried to recall who might have been killed in the explosion.

Gustav waited for the guard to exit the room before he spoke. As soon as the guard exited, Mr. Gustav got down to business.

"Okay, where's my money?" Gustav asked sharply.

"Your money?" Zen replied in an insulted ton. "We made a deal. I'm the one who has been robbed of millions."

"What about my machine?" Gustav asked under heavy distress.

"It's gone," Zen responded in a cold tone.

The answer didn't seem to sit too well with Gustav. He sat there stewing. The realization of his loss began to settle in. He needed something to report back to his superior with, but even he wasn't sure what to make of the events that occurred.

"Okay, then answer me this. What was that thing that showed up?" Gustav asked.

"It's an old project of mine that has suddenly resurfaced," Zen answered.

Gustav looked suspiciously into Zen's eyes, trying to find out if he was telling the truth.

"You created it?" Gustav asked.

"I had a hand in it," Zen replied, trying to protect his exact involvement but at the same time keeping Gustav's curiosity at a peak.

"Okay, okay," Gustav said. "Can you recreate it?"

Gustav hoped that maybe if he could go back to his superior with a group of ultimate fighting machines, then maybe, just maybe, his life would be spared.

"That's what I'm working on," Zen paused.

Gustav sat quietly, looking off into space as if trying to plan out his next move.

"You said there were two deaths?" Zen asked, purposely trying to break Gustav's concentration.

"Yes, one was a Tim Warner, and the other was a Jessica Parsons. She was the old woman you brought in for the experiment, correct?" Gustav responded.

"That can't be." Zen paused again, trying to piece together the possibilities. "She's still alive. I know she is!"

"Regardless, they have you accused of two murders," Gustav answered back, realizing that Zen needed his help just as much as he needed his.

"I tell you this. If you find her, then you'll be able to lure in VoLt."

"You mean the creature?"

"Yes, I guarantee it."

"If I find him, will you help me recreate another one or two for my superiors back home?" Gustav asked.

"I believe I can."

Zen told Gustav the addresses of Miss Parsons with a gleam in his eye that indicated he realized that he might possibly be back in business.

People of all nationalities rushed back and forth from one terminal to the next. Dustin sat and watched as he tried to guess whether the passengers were coming or going. He looked up and saw Jessica approach him as she made her way back from the airline counter. For the first time, he saw her as a twenty-five year old and not the eighty-something year old. She wore blue jeans and a black, turtleneck sweater. He couldn't help but laugh to himself as he realized that it was probably her first pair of blue jeans that she had ever owned.

"You went shopping yesterday, didn't you?" Dustin asked as she got within speaking distance.

"I had to!" she said as she looked down at her jeans as if being a little uncomfortable with dressing to fit her new age. "I guess I have to look the part, as they say. Do I look okay?" she asked self-consciously about her appearance.

"You look great! You look like a twenty-five-year-old," Dustin said as he looked at her again, watching her hair flow down in soft waves. He had never really noticed that she had long, light-brown hair. He could see now why Tim would have been so enamored by her.

They sat down for a couple of minutes while they waited for her plane to board.

"Montana. Can you believe it? Montana," Jessica said with a smile. "I can't want to see the mountains! I have always wanted to see them!"

"You'll get to see them every day," Dustin said.

"Now, are you going to come out to visit?" she asked.

"I'd like to someday. Just kind of have to see how things go around here."

"Well, I put some money into this account," she said as she pulled out a bank deposit slip. "It's for you to use at your disposal."

"Miss Parsons, I can't," Dustin said as he read the amount in the account.

"First, call me Jessica. For crying out loud, we're the same age now," she said as she playfully slapped him on the shoulder with her plane ticket. "Second, Dustin, it's left over from the money Detective Hobbs used to fund this relocation. I want you to have it."

Dustin studied the bank slip.

"With your new duties, it wouldn't hurt to have some money set aside for emergencies," she continued. "And plus, maybe you can squeeze out a trip to Montana to see your family and me."

"Maybe," he said with a smile.

"You have my family's information, right?" he asked.

"Yes, I do. I'm really eager to meet them!" she answered. "When's the last time you saw them?" she asked as he tried to find out more about him.

"Uh, I think it's been about seven years. They traveled over here for a visit," he said. "They are from my mom's side of the family," he explained. "Mom met Dad when she came over to study here in England."

"Have you been to Montana before?" she probed.

"A couple times when I was younger. It is beautiful there," he said.

Jessica gleamed with excitement as she glanced down at her watch.

"Oh my goodness. I better be going if I'm going to get through customs and catch my flight," she said.

They both stood up as Jessica bent down and grabbed her carry on and threw the strap over her shoulder.

"I hope they don't lose my luggage. I haven't had a chance to wear my new clothes yet," she said with a smile.

She reached over and gave Dustin a hug. They squeezed each other tight, and then she finally let go.

"Take care of yourself," she said as she patted his chest, trying to fight back the sudden appearance of tears.

"Will do. You do the same," he replied. "Keep in touch, and tell my aunt and cousins hello for me."

"Will do!"

She reached over as kissed him on the cheek and quickly stepped away. Dustin stood still while he watched Jessica jump in line to go through the airport security. He watched her place her carry-on bag on the conveyer belt and then hand the security agent her boarding pass and passport. She walked through the screener and grabbed her belongings and began to make her way down the terminal. Just as she was about out of sight, she stopped and turned around.

Finding Dustin, she blew him a kiss good-bye and waved. Dustin raised hand, pretending to catch the kiss, then returned the wave. Then Jessica disappeared down the terminal. Once she was out of sight, Dustin reached up to wipe the tear away.

He tried to grasp what his heart felt. He did not expect to have this feeling overcome him. Maybe it was just the fact that he had to say good-bye to a friend that knew things about him that no one knew. Maybe it was the realization that he said good-bye to someone before he had the chance to let her know everything about himself.

There were many things in his life that he decided to keep buried long before he accepted the youth minister position at the church. But with the recent events, he might have needed a friend to confide in. Now that friend was leaving. He could feel the loneliness begin to creep in.

It had been a month since Jessica left for the states when Dustin received her first letter in the mail. He reread it again for the third time that evening. He was happy to hear from her, and he was eager to write back, but he couldn't tonight.

Locking the door of his quarters, he put on his new, black, spandex runner pants that seemed to fit rather well. Dustin knew that the material would expand with him when needed. He proceeded to stretch his legs, testing the mobility of the new attire. Then he threw on the old, black, hooded cloak.

Dustin looked down at the small Post-it note that had an address scribbled on it as it rested on his dresser. A couple of days before, he had been informed by a new student in his Bible study about a friend who would be regularly beaten by his drunk father every night that he came home from the pub. This would be the first domestic situation that he would encounter, but nonetheless, a treasure of the Lord was in harm's way.

Dustin knelt down and prayed, "Dear Lord, grant me the wisdom and guidance to do your will. Grant me the strength to deal with the demons that I might encounter. In your name I pray, amen."

Then he stood up and placed the gold *V* medallion around his neck as his body transformed into VoLt. He pushed back the dresser and opened the small, secret door. Then he entered and disappeared into the darkness. He left to defend those who prayed and needed help. Their prayers were about to be answered.